MISPLACED LOVE

Misplaced Love

short stories

by

MAGGIE DWYER

For dear Joy
xox

Maggie

TURNSTONE PRESS

Turnstone Press
607-100 Arthur Street
Artspace Building
Winnipeg, Manitoba
Canada R3B 1H3
www.TurnstonePress.com

Turnstone Press gratefully acknowledges the assistance of the Canada Council for the Arts, the Manitoba Arts Council and the Government of Canada through the Book Publishing Industry Development Program.

The Canada Council | Le Conseil des Arts
for the Arts | du Canada

Canadä

Printed in Canada by Friesens
for Turnstone Press.

Original cover art by Julia Breckenreid
Design by Manuela Dias
Author photograph by Boomer Jerritt

National Library of Canada Cataloguing in Publication Data
Dwyer, Maggie.
Misplaced love
ISBN 0-88801-257-8
I. Title.
PS8557.W94M56 2001   C813'.6   C2001-910200-3
PR9199.3.D896M56 2001

for John

ACKNOWLEDGEMENTS

Thanks to George Amabile, Sandra Birdsell, Neil Besner, Patrick O'Connell, Carol Shields and Joan Thomas for encouragement and advice.

Other versions of these stories appeared previously as follows: "After Chernobyl" in *Necessary Fiction*, "Lot's Wife" in *Border Crossings* and *Heart of Wisdom*, "Wrap Your Troubles in Dreams" in *Room of One's Own* and "Once More with Feeling" on CBC Festival of Fiction in 1999.

I would also like to thank the Canada Council for the Arts for their financial support of the 1999 Festival of Fiction.

TABLE OF CONTENTS

"We are never so helplessly unhappy
as when we lose love."
—S. Freud

Lot's Wife

Bernie remembers how he nearly killed Issy Fleigl at the Y. He was down in the locker room, in his boxers, doing a few of the stretches the therapist recommended, when that *shlump* came up behind him and faked a snatch at his privates.

"Just wanted to check your bags," Fleigl snorted.

Bernie menaced him with a few swipes of his towel.

"Don't be so touchy," Issy said. "What you need is to get more out of life. But it's not so easy at our age, is it? Cold showers are no good for the arthritis. Now we have to make do with whatever God leaves to us. *Az och un vey!*"

Clad only in a damp white sheet slung like a sarong below his hairy belly, Fleigl draped a damp arm around Bernie's shoulders and pulled him closer. Bernie shivered with distaste. "Listen to this, *boychik*; I've got a little story for you," Fleigl whispered, his warm breath stirring the grove of coarse white hairs that flourished at the tragus of Bernie's left ear.

"Jake and Becky are celebrating their fiftieth wedding anniversary. They return to the same hotel, the same room where they spent their honeymoon night. At two o'clock in the morning, Jake nudges Becky in bed and says, 'Becky— *derland mir die tzeyner, ich vill dir a beis geben.* Hand me my teeth,' he tells her, 'so I can nibble on you.'" Tears welled up in Fleigl's bulgy eyes and overflowed their discoloured pouches; his hairy belly vibrated fitfully.

"You're a sick man. Can't you get your mind out of the gutter?" Bernie sighed as he pushed off the offensive arm. "At your age, isn't it time for a little dignity?"

"Life is short," said Fleigl. "Don't lose your appetite for it. I could introduce you to a very fine woman . . . if you're interested."

"I am a married man," Bernie snapped and continued dressing.

"Okay, have it your way," Fleigl huffed. "It's up to you, if you want to miss out on Sonia Bregman; it's your funeral. She won't make your pulse race but older women are very grateful, Bernie. The best part is, they never tell, and," he added, accenting his point with a flourish of his index finger, "they never swell."

"Don't insult me," Bernie warned, pulling on his over-coat. "I don't want to meet anyone. I don't need any of your favours." He picked up his club bag and walked toward the door.

"She doesn't wear shorts and she doesn't play mah-jong," Fleigl sang out to his departing back.

Bernie wheeled around and started back toward Fleigl, his eyes glinting with rage. "Look here, Mr. Matchmaker, keep your beak out of my business, you," he sputtered, "you puffball." He jabbed at Fleigl's ugly mug, his finger almost scoring a hit on the nasty-looking wen that dominated the left cheek.

That encounter soured Bernie's day. He muttered curses and unflattering sentiments about Fleigl and his ilk all the way over to Main Street. The northbound bus was crowded with forlorn-looking Natives, young mothers with squalling children and other *alter kuckers* like himself. He stomped off the bus at Pritchard Avenue and dove into the moist fragrant air of the florist's shop. His order was ready: twelve luscious long-stemmed red roses like those he had given his valentine every year for the past forty-six. Every year, even the lean ones.

At the Home, Sarah was waiting for him, sitting with her pal Mimi Kates in her usual spot between the potted palms in the solarium, next to the blue-tiled fountain, which gurgled softly. Theirs was a quiet corner avoided by those whose faulty waterworks made sitting in close proximity to the fountain intolerable. Ginger-haired Mimi, an inveterate do-gooder, was the *maven* and a lifetime member of Hadassah, whose meddlesome ways were a trial to many. As usual, a sheik's ransom in gold and diamonds decorated her webby neck and liver-spotted hands. The buttons of her ancient lime-green crimpoline pant suit strained over her majestic shelf of bosom. She was a soft-hearted old girl who doted on Sarah and did her many small favours, which Bernie appreciated deeply.

"Look who it is, Sarah," she warbled as Bernie approached.

Hat in hand, he bowed slightly at the waist and held the long white florist's box out to Sarah.

"My goodness," she exclaimed, "Is that for me?"

Mimi hauled herself to the edge of the seat and, using the arms of her chair for leverage, launched her rotund body erect on arachnid legs.

"Don't go, dear," pleaded Sarah, who was still cradling the unopened box of flowers. "I'd like you to meet my friend." She smiled radiantly and with a delicate blush put her white hand out to Bernie.

"Both of you are so good to me." She extended her left hand to Mimi and drew all four hands together, raising Bernie's and Mimi's to her soft cheeks.

Once again, Bernie suffered the bitter charade of introductions to Mimi. As always, he yearned for their fine bright love, now dimmed, and their inaccessible past, now shriveled to a husk. Where did it go, he wondered, all those years Sarah and I spent *kibbitzing* behind the counter in our store? The customers loved her. People still ask after her. How is your darling wife? they ask. Terrible, terrible, what can happen to a person.

Today, a flicker of recognition showed in Sarah's eyes as he gave his name. Though he continuously noted such signs, he no longer felt hopeful. All the doctors had counseled him to remain detached. Don't feel you must come here every day, they said; we do all that can be done for her. He had the rest of his life to live, they said.

The rest of his life. That sounded like a cruel joke. Those unnumbered years stretching ahead, in a fearsome and arid perspective he dares not face. At the turn of the year, he had felt such anger when the cantor raised his voice and sang, "On Rosh Hashanah it is written, on Yom Kippur it is sealed; How many shall pass on, how many come to be; who shall live and who shall die; who shall see ripe age and who shall not." What about his Sarah? What about those who just exist? At that he had stood, folded his *talis*, walked out of the *shul*, and never returned.

Every afternoon, in their imitation of life, he sits with Sarah until twilight. He brings her news of their children and grandchildren. Stories of their older son, Nathan, who married money, living with his cool thin princess and their children in the palace in Tuxedo with their Filipino slave. Stories about Max, their son the lawyer-turned-land-developer, and his barren lawyer wife, Judith, the *Bal Tshuva*, and the very important work they do. More stories about their little Rosie, the nutritionist, and the recipes she sends him. How she tries to make a cook out of him, who has never so much as boiled water for tea. He makes jokes about how she tells him to think of cooking as simple chemistry.

Sarah is an accepting listener but her responses are cryptic. "I don't want to burn myself," she says, and later, "I was gone; I found myself. I have to go back again. Everything bang. Right out of me."

He tells her stories to affirm their lives, to pass the afternoons, to fill the air between them. "We've come this far," he coos and gives her hand a squeeze.

A narrow crescent of bone-coloured moon hovers over the North End as Bernie Rubinov shivers along Polson Avenue past tiny yards knee deep with snow. He loathes these mid-February twilights and the empty house he must go home to. Of course, today the door gives a real struggle to remind him that he forgot to oil the locks before the winter set in. He mutters a potent imprecation that doesn't work as well as oil, but he's too late with that and besides, a few well-chosen words can give enormous satisfaction.

The door gives up and Bernie shuffles in, the wind digging at his back. Dying light outlines the bulky iceberg shapes of his appliances. The warning light on his small freezer glows rubyred. He dumps the brown paper bag he is carrying onto the square kitchen table and opens the ceiling light.

After a few moments of blinking and dabbing at watery eyes, first with bare cold fingers, then with the softer ends of his red plaid scarf, he goes to the cupboard over the sink, reaches in and lifts down a bottle of rye whiskey and a shot glass. He pours himself a measure and tosses it back with a shiver. He bangs the glass down, turns, sags into the counter, and briskly chafes his hands. As the whiskey warmth hits him, he unbuttons his worn sheepskin coat and vigorously rubs his firm paunch.

"Now we're talking, buddy," he hoots, and flips on the small colour TV on his kitchen table. The face and voice of the pretty local anchorwoman warm up the room. Bernie pays no attention to the newscast. It's trouble everywhere; she doesn't have to tell *him*. He sets the contents of his grocery bag out on the plastic tablecloth. Three white styrofoam containers from the nearby deli. He fetches a spoon and begins to slurp up thick bean and barley soup. Bernie still hasn't removed his coat; he pushes his astrakhan hat back off his forehead and drinks the last of the soup from the container.

Just then, the wall telephone rings. His response is gruff and indignant. "Who is this?" It's his youngest daughter, calling from Vancouver.

"Rosie! *Bubele*, it sounds like you're in the next room, sweetheart. How's the weather by you?" Edgily, in a rising tone, he adds, "on the coast? Rain, that's wonderful. . . .

Flowers too. You got all the luck. . . . Here? It's winter. Yeah, with a capital W. What can we do about it? Nothing.

"Yes, sweetheart, I'm just finishing my dinner. No, you're not interrupting. Well, yes, you are interrupting but this type of interruption, I don't mind. I know you don't want to shampoo my rugs.

"What am I eating? Let me tell you; I got a nice soup, some fish, a beautiful *kugel*." He casts a sheepish glance at the freezer's red eye.

"No. Rosie, no. I still got lots of the food you made for me. It keeps so wonderful in the freezer. I'm telling you, if the Queen of England drops over here, I could give her a nice dinner."

He is astounded that she is content to live there crowded up under those mountains. He doesn't understand why she moved away or why on earth her brother Max and his Judith endure Ottawa. The winters there are not much better. Only Nathan, his eldest, stayed in Winnipeg. He went into the computer business with his father-in-law, Sol Finegold.

"What do you mean have I decided about California? I told your brother, I'll think about it. I'm still thinking."

Nathan and that *farmisht* wife of his, Lisa, want him to leave Sarah behind in Winnipeg to go and spend Passover with them at a fancy resort in California. Lisa has also asked Rosie and Max and Judy. She sent to Bernie's home address glossy brochures showing the steamy spa full of naked women mummied in herbs and cellophane wrap, the golf courses, the horseback riding, the tennis and the world-class shopping. It was not for believing: horseback riding and *matza* mixed all in together. He didn't know what kind of Jew went to a spa for *Pesach*. Elizabeth Taylor, maybe.

"Okay, okay. I said I'll think about it. I know, I know. The deadline is at the end of the month. I am not shouting. I caught a little cold and I don't hear so good these last few days. It's nothing, darling. Sorry. Anyway, I'm feeling better already, really, just talking to you.

"No, I will not bother the doctor; he's a busy man. I went to the Y for a *shvitz* before lunch. That really fixed me up. No, I am feeling beautiful now. You should see me; I could make Burt Reynolds very jealous.

"Happy Valentine's Day to you too.

"Yes, I saw your mother this afternoon. She's the same, lovely as always. No change.

"Thank you, sweetheart. Thank you for calling."

After he says good-bye to Rosie, Bernie goes into the bedroom and takes the wedding photo down from the bureau. He dusts off the glass with the tail of his shirt. "A lot of water under the bridge, kiddo," he whispers, "a whole lot."

The first time Bernie saw his Sarah was in 1941. The first day of October. In those days he thought he was a real *macher*, working for Hershfield at the scrap yards on McPhillips. Twenty years old and full of pepper. That summer Ted Williams batted .400. War was raging and, all of a sudden, scrap metal was a very important commodity. It didn't sound half-bad when people asked why he wasn't going over the pond to give that *meshugener* Hitler what for. Not that he didn't want to. He knew he could tear that monster apart with his bare hands.

You had to hand it to the military, he always said. They got the whole country organized overnight. Everybody had a little job that added up to the big job of winning the war. All the *goyim* were saving up the fat from their bacon and the Jews, the *shmaltz* from their chicken soup. They had to deliver it back to their butchers. The government's newspaper ads claimed it was an essential component in building bombs. Be a munitions maker right in your own kitchen. Out of the frying pan, into the firing line. But Bernie knew for a fact that at the very same time, they were throwing away tins of fat on army bases. Maury Binder saw it with his own eyes. That's what went on in the war; everybody was busy.

The first time Bernie saw Sarah was at the Yom Kippur dance. She was dressed in pale rose silk and her blonde hair was pinned up like Betty Grable's. She was with another man, a tall, good-looking RCAF sergeant in snappy dress uniform, a blaze of medals and ribbons on his left breast. Her brother Max, he found out later.

Bernie was smitten. As soon as Harold Green's orchestra started playing "Don't Sit Under the Apple Tree With Anyone Else But Me," he cut in on them. Looked her right in her blue eyes and said, this could be our song. He couldn't explain it. It was something like being drunk, but better. He was only glad she felt it too. He told himself that the ways of fate cannot be understood. It is better to surrender than to question. They had a good life together; it was a perfect match. They enjoyed everything, even used to get pretty frisky. Just to think about it now makes him glow. They wanted to be together all the time. They were.

On Friday evenings, he goes to eat dinner with his sister. Rachel, or Rae, as she likes to be called, is a bulky, plain-speaking, avowed feminist who looks and dresses like her heroine, Golda Meir. Always the girl in sensible shoes. At sixty-two, she's winding down a long teaching career at the Yiddish day school where her Party membership has always been an asset. Rae's only child, a son, was stillborn. She had married Moe Glantzer, a handsome gambler who specialized in longshots. Moe lived to bet and to dress well. He led her what everyone said was a terrible life. Even when they were flat broke and being hounded by creditors, he kept buying new dress shirts. He used to hide them in the garage and try to sneak them into the house past Rae's eagle eye. As soon as she recovered from the pregnancy, she threw Moe and his shirts out. Holus bolus.

These two survivors bring each other up to date over their Friday night chicken. Bernie shows her the brochures from the spa. "Look," he says, "it includes: daily synagogue services, free nutritional analysis, all meals *Glatt Kosher*, thirty minutes from the ocean. Does that sound like a *ganze metsiah* or what?"

"Maybe to Lisa," Rae answers, "who only knows to shop and exercise. She wouldn't have to change a dish." She's always found Lisa strange, with her black clothes, sour face and those two pale children with the fake names. Bree and Krystall. Why she spends all her time to keep herself like a doll with the long fingernails and all is more than Rae can ever understand. She wants to shake Lisa and scream at her, "Get a life!" Sure, she's pretty, Rae agrees, but that's all she's got.

"How do you understand it? And the way she wants to stay down in California with her parents all the time instead of being here with her wonderful Nathan?"

"You're asking me?" Bernie sighs. "All I know is, we're a long way from Minsk."

After dinner, Rae gets out the cards for gin rummy. They sit with their slippered feet tucked under an ancient bridge table. Sue Ellen and J.R. squabble in the background. Bernie tells her about Fleigl's joke and his asinine proposition: how insulted he was, how his blood was jumping, how he nearly killed him.

"Good thing his rug is glued on. I'd like to have seen it sail clear across the locker room. Did you make those *varenikes* yourself? From Mama's recipe? I thought so; they melt on the tongue."

"Stay away from Sonia Bregman," Rae cautions. "Her dentures clack like castanets."

"What's the matter with these widows?" grumbles Bernie, sorting his hand into suits. "Can't they even wait until the body is cold? Is it nerves?" he puzzles, "or the menopause?"

"No, not that. She's way past menopause; I'm sure she's at least sixty. Wasn't she a Waldman? I think I went to school with her sister, Fanny Drache. You know those long-faced Waldmans; they lived over the Chinese laundry on Selkirk. The father was a *luftmensch*. He was in drygoods, he was in men's suiting, he was in wholesale, he was in retail. Nothing worked out. Fanny used to say her parents were so poor they didn't pay rent—they moved. They lived on Selkirk, on Powers, on Magnus. I think the mother was a Fleigl, Issy's aunt. No, it couldn't be menopause. Menopause is when you wake up at four in the morning and start putting makeup on your face. As for the teeth, it's obvious; her dentist is a real thief."

"Baruch, will you look at the dress on that Pamela," she says, waving her fan of cards at the TV. "I heard those gowns cost three thousand dollars each."

"Gin," crows Bernie. "Again."

"If I had a dress that cost three thousand dollars, I'd want to be reincarnated so I could come back and wear it in another life."

After "The National," Bernie pushes his teacup away and gets ready to struggle home. At the door, Rae presses a jar of soup into his hands. She urges him to pull his hat down and his scarf up. He declines her offer of a spiked cane to battle the ice underfoot. He pretends to be impatient. It is the only time of the week that he doesn't feel lonely.

Tonight, bless heaven, the seven blocks from Matheson down to Polson are free of muggers, and Bernie makes it back to his doll house with ease. He is sinking deep into dreamless sleep when the phone starts ringing. It takes him seven rings to pull on his tired robe and *shlep* out to the kitchen, slippers flopping off his skinny white ankles. Where did he leave his glasses? He can't think. On the eleventh ring he lifts the receiver to hear a scolding voice.

"Dad, when are you going to put an extension in your bedroom? It takes you so long to answer."

"I had to find my glasses."

"Dad, you don't need bifocals to answer the phone."

"It's after eleven o'clock here, mister. Don't argue with an old man. I know what I need."

Max is calling to find out if Bernie has made his mind up about spending Passover in California. Big shots like him and wife Judith need plenty of advance notice so they can arrange their complicated lives.

"Aren't you at all worried about what your mother will be doing?" Bernie demands. "Aren't you at all concerned where she is going to sit for the *Seder*?"

"Pop, I know it's hard for you, but we have to be realistic. It doesn't do your health any good to live the way you do. You need to relax, get a little sunshine. You won't be missed. Mama doesn't know who we are any more. She doesn't even know who you are."

"She doesn't even know who I am. Is that a fact? She doesn't even know who I am." The veins at his temples begin to throb. "Well, let me tell you something, Mr. Know-It-All, I know who she is."

Bernie continues to sputter as he clangs the receiver down and shuffles back to bed. For forty-five minutes by the digital clock, he thrashes around in his sheets. Extra blankets can't warm him. He doesn't drift off until he lays out the spare pillows on Sarah's side and wraps himself around them. Then he falls into the bottomless dark.

When he lands he is right out in front of the house in his shirtsleeves. All the houses in the neighbourhood look abandoned, their windows empty, their doors ajar. Everywhere snow had been, now there is fine white sand. The moon's full face hangs low in the south. He gets up and strikes off toward the Home. His steps are light as floss and he follows the moon's path eagerly. At Main Street, the sand stretches toward the prairie horizon in endless undulations. The Home is entirely gone; where it stood, a mighty golden sphinx towers on a claw-legged throne beside a woman. The sand all around is covered with dry bones gleaming in the silvery light. With another look, he sees that it is Rae's doughty head on the sphinx.

"Baruch," she says, "I'm glad you're here. Give a look here to your Sarah." She nods toward the woman. "I have watched over her this whole night. Go close to her that you may see she is your wife." As Bernie moves toward Sarah, the sphinx unfolds its great dark wings and beats off across the sand, lifting higher with each stroke.

"Rae," he wails after her, "don't leave me here alone."

She turns to circle low over his head. "Next year, Bernie," she croaks, "Next year in Jerusalem."

With a sob, Bernie, his heart still turned to love, steps closer to embrace his wife. His lips touch her smooth cheek and taste salt.

"Sarah," he whispers, "I'm here, I'm here."

After Chernobyl

LIZ GLANCES UP AT HER DAUGHTER'S BEDROOM WINDOW, A rectangle of opaque glare reflecting the midafternoon sun. Erin is up there. Liz imagines her, splayed out on the bed with her headphones on. Plugged into the Dead Kennedys. Her thin body clad in tight black jeans and a T-shirt. Her ugly high-top runners dangling over the foot of the bed. Her spiked hair a stark halo on the pillow.

Liz swirls the half-melted ice in the dregs of her vodka and tonic and belts it back. She ignores her aching teeth, chomps down hard on the ice and lime. Now she wishes she'd gone to Philly with Des. Never mind the five days of strained conversation with his mother. Never mind that she's already seen the Liberty Bell. Anything would beat being held captive by the three H's.

Heat, haze and humidity envelop the city in a suffocating cocoon. She's found no respite on the deck. The wind chimes are still. She peels her back off the plasticized cover of her chaise and sits up to spit the shreds of lime back into her glass. The scent of lime usually triggers desire, reminds her of her Mexican honeymoon. Now, because Des is away, it's a trigger to further annoyance, like the trickle of sweat that runs down the slope of her trim tanned belly.

Liz scowls and slips her toes with their hot pink polish into her old wedgies, the ones she wears when Des is not around. She steps through the glass patio doors into the artificial cool of the house. It has a dull exhausted odour that she imagines is like the air inside a coffin. Their refrigerator hums a monotonous refrain.

The door to Erin's room is ajar and, yes, she is there, lying almost as Liz imagined her. She's wearing Josh's jean jacket, the one with the encircled capital A on the back. It's the nucleus of her wardrobe these days; its lapels covered with buttons that advertise his current affiliations. The one constant in these constellations, his north star, is a "ban the bomb" pin. Liz sees that button as an omen, an emblem of Josh's centre and takes comfort in the odd fact that it's the same emblem Des wore when they met. Of course, Des says this is false comfort: SUPA is dead and most of today's kids are nihilists. *Carpe diem*, sweets, he says. We're here today, could be long gone tomorrow.

Liz fears that Des is right, though she doesn't want to admit it. Philosophy is not her strong suit. She ignores life's black holes; for her, they don't exist. She's the cockamamie optimist; he's the hardboiled skeptic.

IT'S BEEN THIS WAY since their beginning. In October of 1967 Des bounded through the door of the draft resisters' office on Spadina where Liz was labouring over a letter that contained a counterfeit promise of work to another Young American who didn't want to serve his country. She saw Des glance at her newly liberated breasts under her limp Indian cotton *kurta* and she flipped her dark long hair forward to shield them. She'd noticed him before, at the centre of the office's politics, where his reasoned views often prevailed over the hot-voiced rhetoric of the Maoists. Handsome as Sgt. Pepper, a brilliant law student and author of a popular column in the street newspaper, *Guerilla*, he became their Solomon.

On bookshelves that held the collective's library stood a bust of Che Guevara. A Marine deserter, code-named Mick, had constructed it from a styrofoam wig stand, acrylic paint and human hair, topped by the trademark beret. This lurid gargoyle was the collective's main source of inspiration: they stashed their dope inside its hollowed head.

Des tucked the bust under one arm and pulled Liz to her feet with his free hand.

"Come on," he called. "Hurry. The pigs are coming." He helped her drop to the flat roof of the Maple Leaf Laundry and tossed Che down to her. They duck walked across the roof, jumped to the alley and waltzed through the kitchen doors of the New Moon Gardens. Des perched Che on the jukebox, leaving him to brood over their giggles and won ton soup. Liz remembers how cozy their red vinyl booth was. How handsome Des looked (though then she said groovy). How she wanted him right away.

Two nights later, they made candlelight love on the waterbed in his apartment upstairs from the Cawthra

Square commune. Within a week she moved in, bringing her stereo, Ginsberg, her tortoise cat, her dressing table, forty-seven kinds of makeup (pots of creamy colour and cakes of pressed powder for lips and eyes, vials of perfume, a small earthen jar of kohl, scented bath oils), sixteen cartons of books (chiefly paperbacks), two brown corduroy bean bag chairs, her collection of dolls (fifty-six in number), her tie-dyed bed sheets, feathers, beads, bits of lace and a rainbow of clothes. They've been a couple ever since. A fact predicted by dark-eyed Ava, Liz's tightest friend at the time. The trines could not be more harmonious, Ava gushed; you're so together, you two. Des, an airy Gemini and you, a fiery Sagittarius; you'll always need each other.

LIZ WALKS BY Erin's door and into the master bedroom. She takes a silent inventory of the moments from their history captured in the forest of framed photos on the top of their burled walnut highboy. A swell of love washes her calm as she surveys these frozen scenes. Des smiles consistently from frame to frame.

Liz heads down the hallway to fetch a towel from the linen cupboard. As she passes Erin's door she notes that, as far as she can tell, Erin hasn't moved in the last twenty-four hours. Des's flight left at noon on Friday. Yesterday. Mr. Schenley, the principal at Erin's school called Liz around two in the afternoon. Were she and Mr. O'Brien aware, he asked, that their daughter had cut her afternoon classes for three consecutive Fridays?

Actually, he droned on, a number of the staff had expressed concerns about Erin. She seemed bored with her courses. Even her art classes. Recently completed assignments were well below her usual level. He wondered politely if there were any difficulties at home that they should be aware of?

Liz winced, her vocal control flip-flopping as she angled her way out of the conversation. She fended off further questions with promises to discuss the matter with her husband and daughter. And, yes, she did appreciate his concern. Liz set the receiver down carefully, anger infusing the gesture with precision. Anger gave way to fear and she began to shiver violently.

"Mother, we are talking about a spare and a double art class. Don't get yourself all fuzzed up about it."

That was the only response Liz managed to pry out of Erin and it perplexed Liz. Why, if you had asked her, even a week ago, whether she and her daughter were close, she would have answered confidently: yes, Erin tells me everything. Not. Not every thing.

Not since Josh.

Erin's old friend Sarie had introduced them: favourite cousin meet best friend. Josh Silver was camping out with Sarie's family for February while his parents chased the sun down to Trinidad. The two friends flitted around him, offering Coke and pizza. Listen to this, they crooned as the tone arm eased down on "Baby You're A Rich Man." They bopped around lip-synching the words.

"The Beatles are so totally *pêche.*"

"Yeah, they are really cool!"

"They're such complete babes! Aren't they, Josh?" they wheedled.

"*Peche?*" he puzzled, "is that something you put on your hair?"

"No," they chorused.

"Is it some new dessert?"

"No," Sarie giggled, "it's peachy: you know, and like in French—it's *pêche*. It's our new word."

"The word of the week or the word of the weak ... er sex?"

"Don't be a stinker, Josh," Sarie warned.

He sprawled back on Des's lazyboy, his leather-clad legs crossed at the ankles, his motorcycle boots aimed at the ceiling.

He looks like an arrogant young god, Liz thought. She had come to tell Erin that she was going to run out to the liquor store and pick up some wine. She chatted with Sarie and Erin about their school musical and then, to include Josh, asked if he had heard from his parents.

"My parental units? No doubt, they're fine. I hear the weather in Trinidad is divine," he sniggered. An empty smile lingered on his El Greco face. He reached back to clasp his hands behind his head. That's when she noticed thin strips of white cloth wrapped around his wrists. Erin said she didn't know why Josh had his wrists bandaged. She wouldn't dream of invading his privacy by asking. Yes, she agreed that it was kind of a weird thing to do. But like it's still a free world, isn't it? And does everything have to mean something?

"Honey, don't sweat the small stuff," Des counseled. "It's just his shtick. Kids get off on trying different looks. No big deal. Remember beads, headbands, body paint. I'm not crazy for this dude either. He's into film, video, whatever. Something they see as avant-garde. He's eighteen years old. Out of Erin's league. But completely.

"Honey, it's just clothes. He's not about to become a

permanent fixture around here." Des slipped his arms around her waist and pulled her to him, saying that he remembered some pretty foxy outfits she'd put together. "Remember that tight fringed purple suede vest you had? I think it was cut down to about here," he purred, tracing a deep outline over her cleavage.

ERIN HAD HEARD her mother pad down the hallway. She snapped her lids shut behind the dark glasses and let her mouth go slack. The tape in her Walkman was over so she heard Liz's hesitation in the hallway like a skipped beat. She was thinking of the refrain still singing in her head: *I heard the dance remix and I'm not going to be all right.*

When her mother moved on, the sharp pains in her chest came back. Splintered edges ground together like ice floes so she concentrated on breathing light and high up. She could get away from it for a few minutes by pretending that she was adrift. Like a cartoon man on an island with one palm tree. She didn't know that things would change so. She hadn't meant to sleep with Josh or anyone so soon. It was the way he was. It got her all jazzed up He was lying there with his head on her stomach. He rolled his face into her belly and said, "Oh baby, I love your chromosomes." And his warm breath made her give in to it.

Sarie phoned her early yesterday morning to say that her father had to take Josh to the emergency really late on Friday night. For some unknown reason he had totally freaked.

They took the subway down to the Clarke on Saturday morning but when they got there, the nurses said he couldn't have any visitors. They could hear him shouting "Nelson Mandela, I put out my hand to you," from somewhere down the hall.

LIZ STEPS RIGHT UNDER the shower's pulsing massage, pulling ragged gulps of steamy air in through her mouth. She focuses on the tension in her shoulders, willing it out of her body. With Erin so distant, her radar is on red alert. She reviews the past weeks, screening for clues. Last month, after the blowout at Chernobyl, Erin began dressing in black (like Josh) and sleeping in his jacket. On weekends, the two of them, thin and intense, were busy shooting their video interviews of street people. The real news, according to Erin, life at the edge of the abyss.

Balancing on her right leg, Liz draws her left foot up and runs a pumice stone over the sole. The soapy stone skitters away from her and crashes down on her baby toe. Cursing the sharp pain, she shifts her weight onto her left leg and howls, "Damn you, Josh!" She jerks the water off and slips down to sit on the cool tiles. She covers her eyes and heaves soundless, dry sobs, her blood pounding, hard surf in her ears. Now Josh is the enemy. Like a sly invader, he is a rogue cell who has shifted their focus onto his dark nucleus. He's got to go, she decides, willing him to slip away like a thief in the night. Visualizing Josh as a thief raises another possibility. The one, Liz knows, she has avoided all along. The possibility that Erin and Josh may already be lovers. Would that explain the silences? The missing Friday afternoons?

The phone rings as she towels herself. It was Des.

"Hey, babe," he begins, "what's shaking?"

"Des. How did you know I needed to hear your voice?"

"Where we're concerned, honey, I'm psychically attuned. What's the problem?"

"It's Erin. The minute you left town, all hell broke loose. Mr. Schenley called here yesterday to tell us that she's been cutting school on Fridays for weeks now. I am furious because I didn't have a clue she'd been doing this." Her voice cracks. "She won't talk to me. She slipped out somewhere with Sarie before lunch. I grounded her for the weekend as soon as she got home. Now she's holed up in her room. Incommunicado. The weather is totally filthy and I can't think. I may be getting a migraine."

"Put her on the phone, will you? Maybe I can get something out of her."

Liz summons Erin to the phone, then retreats to the kitchen where she thumps a few dishes around and mixes another vodka to distract herself. More than ten minutes pass before Erin calls her to pick up the kitchen extension.

"Liz? Look, sweetheart, she's okay. This has to do with Josh. She's been going with him to his therapy sessions. She says he's very depressed and she wants to make sure he gets there. She sits and waits for him."

"Is she sleeping with him?"

"Christ, I don't know. I didn't ask. How could I get into that over the phone? I doubt it. Not if he's practically suicidal."

"Yes. You're right, Des," she says. "Yes, I'd know if she was. I mean I'd know if she wasn't."

"Whatever. Look, sweets, I'll see if I can get a late flight out on Monday right after the barbecue. That's the soonest. You girls hold tight until I get home.

"Mom needs me here for her Memorial Day do. There's heavy weather on this end too. She's coming to terms with Patrick's death and the whole Nam thing. She told me she wants us to have the Vermont house and you know that it was always supposed to go to Pat."

"I miss you, Des," she whispers.

"Me too, babe. Me too."

ERIN PADS INTO the kitchen on bare feet, slips her arms around Liz. She's dreamed that she found Josh and her mother making out on the deck and the weird thing was they didn't seem to understand why she was upset. All she can say is, "I need a hug."

"What are you thinking about, Mumsie?"

"I miss your papa."

"Me too. Let's tune the ball game in and pretend he's in the den."

Erin's suggestion about the ball game is right on. The sonorous voices of the announcers fill the house with a rhythm as satisfying as a lullaby and comfort like unseen radiation seeps in through every pore.

The Beautiful Inclination

Leave it at the beautiful inclination.
—Ford Maddox Ford

Matt sat across the kitchen table from Lisa. Safe at home. A pot of tea on the brew between them. Calm and quiet since their reunion at the airport. Neither one upset that his flight was an hour late. They'd passed pale comments on the weather in Washington versus Winnipeg's as they navigated familiar streets lined by bare-limbed trees. How easily they shouldered the yoke of domestic relations. Welcomed it. The weight shared of years that went bone deep.

"Tell me," she asked, "what was the best thing?" This question was part of their ritual when either returned from a trip they had not shared.

The question's converse—what was the worst—was no

longer posed. Not since that day, early in their life, when he replied, "Being away from you."

Their exchange was reduced to the intimate verbal shorthand of the long marrieds. Now at the appropriate juncture, she would say, "And?"

He would reply, "Yes."

The best thing, Matt said, was his discovery at the National Archives Rotunda, of a letter written in a fine, clear hand by the then twelve-year-old Fidel Castro to President Roosevelt. Young Castro wrote to offer congratulations on Roosevelt's election victory, which news he had heard on his new radio. The young man asked the President to send him ten green American dollars for, he continued, "I have never seen such a thing as ten green American dollars." Fidel apologized for his poor English and opined that the President's Spanish probably was not very good either. In closing he offered to take Roosevelt on a tour to the best mines in Cuba to obtain ore to build his *sheaps*, which he crossed out and with a broad, definite stroke corrected to *ships*.

Matt did not wait for her to ask that second question tonight. As the last word fell from his lips, he leaned forward slightly and said yes, yes, and always yes.

What he remembered most clearly about looking at Castro's letter was the way Joanne's breasts had settled on the top of the glass display case as she leaned forward to read the text. Two average regulation issue breasts covered by the white, white linen of a tailored shirt. She had pinned a delicate cameo brooch at her throat.

The light in the rotunda was soft, indirect. The museum guards maintained an atmosphere of deliberate reverential hush that made Matt feel guilty for thinking about breasts and not about the Declaration of Independence or the Bill of Rights. In the murals painted on the dome of the rotunda, the founding fathers presided over the nation's icons like prim schoolmarms. Matt found it hard to think of sex and George Washington and his wooden false teeth simultaneously. Anyway, he suspected this would be classified as an un-American activity. So forget history, he told himself.

It was the cigar he had noted first. The beautifully full red-painted lips clamped around a long black stogie. Joanne Moore was leaning forward, head canted to the right, sucking up a light from the match cupped in the hands of his pal, Jake Warren. She had wide dark eyes and an unfashionably full sort of figure. The kind that used to be likened to an hourglass. Or in my case, she quipped, make that three-quarters of an hour. She wasn't more than five feet tall. Her black sheath dress was cut low with little bands for sleeves. This set off her shoulders. And her white face. Her dark hair was twisted back in a French roll.

Jake looked up and caught Matt's eye across the herd of reception guests crowding the embassy's Canada room. Matt nodded in reply and inched his way toward them.

Jake put an arm around both of their shoulders and turned them so they were huddled face to face. He introduced them. "Joanne—Matt. Matt—Joanne. You've already received advance reports on each other." They all smiled, eager to please.

"Matt, let me get you a drink."

"Me too, darling. Please."

"I say," Jake said in a Pythonesque tone, "isn't that your fourth glass of champagne?" He ran the back of his index finger up the side of her neck and tugged gently on her right ear lobe—"just checking, old thing. You know accurate records are a big deal here."

"It's okay, *mon cher*, it's Canadian juice. Not nearly so intoxicating as the French. After all, darling, this is the usual quiet celebration by sweet little Canada." She tilted her chin up and blew a wavery blue ring of smoke above their heads.

"What did you do to get invited here?" she asked, turning to Matt as Jake went in search of drinks.

"I am the computer geek," Matt said. "I was involved in doing the calculations for the Canadian components. You may have seen the Arm on TV doing little repair jobs in space. It's like a giant screwdriver."

"Don't be so modest," interrupted Jake as he handed them fresh glasses. "You headed the design team for that project. That was major."

The men had been in school together at Upper Canada College in Toronto. At school Jake was all-star, led in everything from sports to singing. No one was surprised at his successes.

"And I," said Joanne, throwing her arms open wide, "*I* am the curator of the all-Canadian art show that no one is looking at."

"Everyone is talking about how clever it is, darling," said Jake.

"Don't patronize me, you art-despising petty bureaucrat," she said in a low, rough voice. "Or try to make a fool of me. Remember what I told you, sweetheart—underdogs have sharp teeth." She snapped her perfect whites at him.

"Let's take this outside, shall we," Jake said. He quickly surveyed the room and then deftly scooped three more fresh glasses of wine from a passing waiter and led the way outside to the courtyard.

They stood in a triangle with Joanne at the apex, her back to the Pennsylvania Avenue traffic. Jake asked Matt the standard questions about his flight and the hotel. Matt asked Jake about the salmon treaty talks he was heading.

"Come on, guys. Don't start talking about fish, 'cause, if you do, I'm going to ride out of here." Joanne handed her glass to Jake. She crossed the courtyard and stepped over the chain and splashed through the pool of water toward the immense sculpture. The squabbling crew of Bill Reid's *The Spirit of Haida Gwaii* gleamed black and mighty.

"I'm going to fly right out of here to never-never land with these spirit guys." She reached over the Wolf's snout for a handhold on the Eagle's wing but slipped and fell on her ass on the bed of stones under the sculpture.

Matt and Jake stood staring at her. She leaned back on her arms, smiled, and tilted her head up as if she were on a beach.

"Come on in," she called. "The water's fine." She began scooping handfuls at their feet.

The men turned to face each other.

"*La Dolce Vita*," Jake said impatiently, "Jesus! She's too much. Do me a huge favour? I've got to go back in there and talk to some people. Will you put her in a cab? Tell her I had to go. She knows. Tell her I'll call her tomorrow." Wineglasses still in both hands he turned, lifted one in salute to Joanne, and walked back into the reception. "See you, sweetie," he called.

"Hey," Joanne called loudly, "hey, don't leave me. Jesus!" She tucked a stray lock of her hair behind her left ear. "Won't anyone help me up?"

Jake didn't look back.

"Woman overboard," she called out. And again. Louder. Fretfully.

"Here's a lifeline, lady." Matt took his tie off and flipped the wide end out to Joanne. He pulled her to her feet. The water was cold and that seemed to sober her up a little. She was sodden and dripping below the waist.

"Thanks, mister." She reached down to wring out the hem of her skirt.

"That's the last we'll see of our old pal Jake tonight. Damn! The amount of time you guys spend talking about fishing is humiliating for women. Why don't men know that?"

She took hold of Matt's lapels to steady herself and draped his tie loosely around his neck. She used the ends to pull his face close to hers and gave him a kiss on each cheek.

"Thank you again." She smiled. "My hero."

Matt smiled and made a slight bow.

"Don't take this the wrong way but I think you really are a nice guy. A steady, dependable, nice guy. Not like some who, if you have any sort of bad luck, seem to become afraid of you. It's true," she nodded. "They try to forget you. And it's worse if they're on the way up and you're not. That's why the bottom is loaded with nice people. Only cream and bastards rise.

"Not everyone understands about the beauty of tragedy." She took off her right shoe and held it up to let the water drain out.

"Not even a goldfish. Too bad. They're my favourites. Besides," she tapped him on the lapel of his jacket with the toe of her shoe, "anything can be beautiful if you say it is. It's all in the slant of your eyes.

"Jake's right to leave me. I know I'm too loud. About five drinks too loud. Last July, he didn't call me for two weeks. That's the longest he's gone. He is a devil of a character. Did you notice his cloven hooves? Like all politicians, he speaks with forked tongue." She chopped through the air with her ruined shoe.

"The happiness market's crashed, baby. So how about a stiletto right through his black heart?"

She leaned forward and rested her head on Matt's chest.

"Excuse me. Please, I didn't really mean that. I'll take it back. This is some fucking Hell." Her eyes shimmered with unspilled tears. "All I want is to be the love of his life. But damn him, he won't let me. I've been making excuses for him so long it's become my major mental vice. Every day I make up my mind to go back to him.

"Is that love? I wouldn't know." She tugged hard on his lapels. "If I have to choose between grief or nothing, I'll take grief. Why can't he be more interested in domestic affairs? Like you. I bet you are a domestic affairs specialist."

Matt reached down and plucked up one of the smallest stones in the pool. It was ovoid, horn coloured, an ancient little thing.

"Here," he said. He took her hand and placed the cool stone in the centre of her palm. It was the size of the pad of her thumb. He closed her fingers over it.

"Keep this. See how your luck will change."

Joanne opened her mouth and carefully placed the stone on the centre of her tongue and closed her lips over it. She tilted her head up as if in prayer and closed her eyes. She stayed motionless for a few seconds.

"Don't swallow," said Matt softly.

She took it out and looked at it quizzically. "I think I've got the feel of it now. Do I put it in my shoe to remind me of this lovely evening?" She glanced at her feet. "I don't think I could walk then. I'll keep it in my pocket. In case. In case I get lost. Then I rub it and you'll appear to rescue me and grant me three wishes."

The toes of her suede shoes were scuffed and shabby with wet. "This is the end for these beautiful shoes too," she said.

"Say, weren't you assigned to take me to my hotel? I'm at the Radisson. It's thataway." She pointed over his right shoulder down Pennsylvania Avenue.

"Let's walk." She put her arm through his and pressed her head against the sleeve of his jacket.

They walked silently, arm in arm, for several blocks west along Pennsylvania Avenue toward the hotel at 13th Street.

"Tell me something interesting," she asked. "Some science thing."

"There's a full moon up there tonight." He was feeling lightheaded, more than the wine would account for. Empty headed. Charged up. Capable of a white-hot phosphorus burn.

"Even though we cannot see it. It's there. You cannot ignore it. Do you know how many full moons we could see in one lifetime? Say you live the proverbial three score and ten. Seventy times twelve. That makes a total of eight hundred and forty possible sightings. Plus the occasional blue moon.

"Tonight, it's high misty indifferent moon. An obscured moon that shines no light on our little corner of the world. How do you think the earth looks from that distance?"

"Let's play hide and go seek with Mr. Moon." She ducked behind him and crouched down to rest her head on his back at his waist.

"Our moon doesn't have a name, does it?" she asked.

"What would you like to call it?"

"Ganymede. But that's taken, isn't it? I don't know.

Ganymede. Ganymede. I like the way that feels in my mouth. I'll never have another love. The man in the moon isn't happy tonight. Me either."

In the elevator, she put her arms around him from behind, snugging up against his back.

"What's this?" she asked. Slipping her hand into his pocket, she whispered, "May I?" and filched his book. He leaned up against the wall of the elevator, arms folded across his chest. He thought about his fantasy life. How it all revolved around hard mechanics. Rarely lust. Occasionally, he thought about his sister-in-law's thighs. How they differed from her twin's. His wife's.

"Who are you?" Joanne smiled mischievously. "What kind of guy comes to a party with a book in his pocket? Are you really that shy?" She thumbed through the pages. "Yikes. This is math!"

She squinted at the cover. "*A Tour of the Calculus* by David Berlicki, or maybe Berlinski." She stuffed the book back into his pocket. "Sounds like a guided tour of Hell."

In front of the door to her room, she paused.

"Are you on your own then?"

Matt did not answer.

"You're not, are you?" She patted his sleeve. "Don't answer. That's okay. As a matter of fact, it's better. I couldn't listen to one more horrible divorce story."

"It's o-kay! Come on in."

She opened the door and walked ahead, slipped her coat from her shoulders, and let it fall to the carpet. She stretched out face down across the nearest bed with her feet hanging over the end and kicked off her ruined shoes. The dye had leached out in black smudges over her toes and around the heels.

"My feet are killing me and I'd ask you to rub them but I think they're smelly and anyway, Einstein, by the way, did I say that I like the way you hold your head? Makes me think of a Renaissance prince. Were you, by any chance, at the court of the Medici family?" She squinted at him. "Perhaps." She raised her head up about six inches. "Oops. Not a good idea," she said. Tiny beads of sweat broke out on her upper lip. "I like your fine grey eyes. So calm and lucid."

She flopped over on her back.

"I wish I could remember something about the stars. Something that would really impress a mathematician. I know you're way too smart for me. I never got math. Mathematician. Magician. It's the same thing.

"Will you please unzip my dress? I hope you don't want sex tonight, baby. I don't think I could perform. Like you guys say. I seem to be a little drunk. Or something."

He steadied himself and pulled down the tab of her zipper parting the dress into equal black halves. She reached behind and with that swift ease women have, single-handedly undid the hooks on her bra. She threw herself back down on the closer of the two double beds, her back to him, forming a slack whorl with thin arms and legs drawn in close to her trunk. Her neckline gaped open. He could see the rounded hills of her breasts and the cups of her bra covering her nipples with snowy lace. On the right one, a thin scar marred her white flesh with a rose-coloured slash that ran under the lace toward her hidden nipple.

Matt sat down on the second bed. He wanted to stay near her for a while longer so he could look at her breasts. Look at them, he told himself, and admire them like any natural phenomena. He had not seen many bared breasts other than Lisa's since they married. He wondered what it would be like to be a doctor, compelled to look at breasts on a daily basis. All sizes, all types, even scarred ones. He wanted to run his tongue along that little scar, follow it back to its source. He was so afraid of the strength of this desire that he began to talk about math.

He took the book out of his pocket and began to tell her that it was not all that difficult and he believed she was very bright and would understand the ideas expressed by the calculus.

"You are speaking a very foreign language." Her voice was drowsy. "My experience with numbers is all negative. The only geometry I know is triangles. I am a qualified expert on love triangles. And, also ... I could tell you about how many small torments can fit into the circle of a wedding ring. Come closer, my dear." She patted the bed. "Here. Here, come to mama."

He walked around behind her and sat down by the curve of her hip.

"I'm afraid of you." He looked into her wide brown eyes "And it's so bad. I don't know how to say what I mean by that."

He didn't know how to express the competing surges of fear and elation he felt at the thought of venturing outside the safe confines of monogamy. Sailing around to the dark side of the moon.

"Do you hate me?"

"Men," she sniffed. "You say you're afraid of me. That usually means you have no idea what to do next." She pulled the pillow over her head.

What he knew was that he was a very few degrees away from coming undone.

"I couldn't do it. I'm too chicken. Here," he took her hand and covered his heart with it. "Feel my heart." Matt held her hand to his chest where the rhythm that was pounding in his ears was seated. "I've never read the manual for adultery." He shook his head. "Wouldn't understand the operating instructions."

"Don't worry. They're written on my body." She inched her way over and put her head down on his thigh.

The best I could do, he thought, is maybe think about asking Jake to let me watch. He wished for grace to battle his temptations. It is one thing to be tempted, another thing to fall.

"I want to do the honourable thing," he said aloud. "For you and me, and for Jake."

"There is no honour where there's sex. You say honour— but what do you mean?"

"I think that when people can agree on the honourable course, the end is love. If not, troubles will result."

"You are losing me, sweetie." She flopped over on her back. "Do you mean the war between the sexes?"

Her face was so white and weary then with all her private battles, he did not speak.

"Don't let's talk about war," she whispered.

She stretched and turned on her side, relaxed into a looser, sleeker posture that conjured the form of a figure-head leading, leading the way across some fierce, unknown sea.

"Guess I slide off now." Matt said.

He straightened the knot on his tie.

"Don't go. Please, stay a little longer. Jake won't call for hours, maybe days. I need some company. Stay until I fall asleep, Mr. Sandman."

When he nodded, she abandoned herself to fatigue with an infant's indolence. Her lips slightly parted, her red lipstick faded to a dull outline.

Matt stayed and read for an hour or more stretched out on the opposite bed. He fenced with Berlinski's thirteen notions about looking at lines to keep from thinking about the geometry on the bed opposite. That did not go so well but he did come up with thirteen ways of looking at a dark-haired woman:

The coordinates of her white legs, her dimpled backside.

The curve of curls, the curl of her ears.

The interface of those lines.

The line that divides his life into before and after.

The essence of a relationship is that things are related.

How to define the shape of her name on his tongue.

A straight line that separates the moment in time when you thought you understood your life from what comes later.

The moment she speaks or just after.

The dimensions of his hope recorded in natural numbers.

The soundwaves of her heartbeat reduced to physics.

The boundaries of love.

The weight of dreams.

The deep property: continuity.

When he thought of continuity, he thought of Lisa. Of love. Of believing in love. In the way d'Alembert was reputed to have said about Faith: *allez en avant et la foi vous viendra.* Go forward and faith will come to you. Life will open. Advice that could be offered with equal validity to students of love or calculus.

The thought of continuity was the thought of Lisa. The

deep property. A rare and valuable commodity. They had made the adjustment of holding all things in common. The story of their marriage was unfolding slowly, revealing its mysteries and satisfactions. The weight of eighteen years of marriage equals X. X equals love. Love is the X factor.

Before he left to go to his own room, he lay down opposite her, curving his body into a C-shape to mirror hers. He stayed there for another ten minutes or so breathing with her rhythm, counting her eyelashes, he ran the tip of his right index finger over the warm pearls that circled her neck. Finally he rolled away and got up to search the closet for an extra blanket to drape over her. He picked her coat up from the carpet and shook out its folds. He slipped his hand into the right hand pocket and felt that smooth stone. He brought it to his lips and rolled it over them like a kiss. He opened his mouth and placed the stone on his tongue and closed his lips over it. The stone felt cool and glabrous against his palate. He removed it with his thumb and middle finger and dropped it into the pocket of his shirt right over his heart.

The next afternoon they went to the National Archives Rotunda. She insisted.

"I want to make it up to you," she said. "Show you some of the precious things at the heart of this town. I behaved badly. And at the embassy party. I'm old enough to know better."

They joined a queue of tourists waiting to see the Declaration of Independence. It was kept in a large glass case flooded with greenish bottom-of-the-sea light. The atmosphere was reverent and the viewers bent over the case humbly as if the founding fathers painted in the dome's murals were watching. Matt walked close to her, deliberately brushing up against her breast.

"Excuse me?" he whispered.

"Give me a good reason," she teased.

He ran his hand down her thigh from waist to hemline. "You did it on purpose, didn't you? Why'd you have to wear this short skirt?"

"Yes. Yes, I'm guilty. I thought you'd like a treat."

"You know, and I do want you to take this personally—you have a gorgeous ass."

"You like it?"

"I do."

"Then we're in luck, aren't we?" She left the queue and moved to look in another display case.

"Have you ever been to Cuba?" He moved behind her as she stood reading Castro's letter through the glass. Close to the soft secret power of her scent. When he pressed up against her back, he could feel the little stone in his shirt pocket. He took it out and savoured the way its warmth transferred to his palm. Then he pulled her closer with his left arm so that her round ass fit perfectly into his belly and as she sighed, he dropped the stone back into her pocket.

"There is a beautiful place between your neck and your shoulder that I almost bit last night. May I?"

She withdrew slightly and turned her head to see if she could read some change in his eyes.

"Well—you think about it."

"You sure want to be bad boy. Don't you? Tell me, am I right? Would you mind very much being seduced?"

"It's not that I mind. It's not that I don't want to see you naked. I do."

He ran his thumbs around the orbits of her eyes and

gently down her cheeks to the corners of her lips. He resisted the urge to force them up into a smile, Though that is what he wanted. To be the one able to make her smile.

Lisa smiled so easily. He remembered that he usually thought, my world goes round because of her. If I sing while I shower, it's because I know I'm going to have breakfast with her.

Where is goodness found, Matt wondered? He'd always thought it was in the continuity they created. That deep property and its inescapable rhythms.

"You are very alluring."

She stood up on tiptoe and whispered right into his ear, "Alluring is good but I want to move up to irresistible."

They stood there by Castro's letter in the glass case, their arms loosely encircling each other's waist.

"No." She patted the sleeve of his tweed jacket. "You're not ready to tango. But thanks," she said. "Thanks for almost everything."

They walked, hand in hand, back to the hotel to wait until it was time to meet Jake for dinner.

"Let's take a little nap," Joanne said and she immediately stretched out on her left side facing the windows. Matt aligned his body to hers. They watched the sky darkening from sapphire through indigo behind the scarlet-leafed trees. A city on fire.

After what he judged might be ten minutes, he nudged

the back of her right knee with his, enjoying the rasp of his corduroy trousers against her nylons.

"Thirsty?" he asked,

"Not now." She reached behind her back, took his hand and curled it under her own across her chest, nestled it over her heartbeat between her breasts.

"Were you asleep?"

"No. I don't like going to sleep. It separates people. Think of it. All we have is in these few moments when we were together and we knew we wanted nothing else. Promise that some night you'll think of me. I imagine that we will be gazing at the same distant star and I'll know that you could tell me exactly how far away it is. It will be the same as the distance between us."

Matt raised himself on one elbow to look at the numerals on the bedside clock. "It's seven," he said. "Jake will be here soon."

"No. We can't get up now. We have to wait until night has fallen."

The sky continued to darken until night closed down and the window reflected the man and woman on the bed and the shadows of the lamps and furnishings of the American standard hotel room.

Matt watched the reflected objects take on sharper definition. The unlit room, its cargo of dark shapes, loomed like the shapes of his dark longings that urged him to touch her. Unruly, frightening longings of which he was slightly ashamed. It's the absence of the thought of love that fails us. Not wickedness but indifference. He knew he was not indifferent. Unfaithful. He thought he knew the truth of that word at last.

And later what he would tell himself happened is this: I

took a brief holiday from who I was. As he thought of how he would remember those two days, his mind was humming with the thought that there are no snow-capped mountains in Cuba. A brief, inscrutable mantra that he could examine from time to time like a favourite souvenir. Take out and rub smooth as a stone.

The Sweet Science

THE LAST TIME I SAW GLORIA WAS AT THE HARD ROCK CAFÉ at the Dome. Months ago. Steve and me were almost finished our regular Friday lunch when she floated over to our table and suckered me with a breathless, "Long time no see, anchorman." Then she saluted me for godsakes.

Never, and I mean never, does this woman fail to unnerve me. So she doesn't know the difference between an anchor and a colour commentator. So she's not an original thinker. She sure knows how to make me sweat.

Something about her reminds me of a volcano. That sounds really stupid but stupid is how I get around women. Consider it a sample of the kind of major-league ideas that occur to me. Right.

She'd got her hair done in a new way. Soft-looking blonde waves piled up on her shoulders. Man, one look at a thing like that and I am shipwrecked. She was wearing this fuzzy sweater the exact same colour as her violet eyes. The neckline was cut in a low vavoom that showcased her Twin Peaks. I don't know who tagged her Gloria, but, boy, they were right on the money.

There's this billboard I pass every day on the way home. Right at Dundas and Dupont. It's a black and white photo of a woman's torso in a bra. A huge white bra with concentric circles of white stitching, floating over the underpass. Every time I look at it, I see Gloria in it.

One time, last spring, it was pouring when I came out of work and there she was at the curb in this really ancient Caddy and I got in with her and we went and had this really hot session on the parking lot outside the McDonald's at Yonge and St. Clair. But I couldn't do it there. I mean—in the middle of the day. There were lots of little kids around. I got the worst case of blue balls ever. So I said please, please just touch it. She put her hand on my guy and said *whatever you want, honey*, in this, this voice. How did she know what I wanted to hear? Gush all over the dash. I had to crawl out of there backwards, gasping like a fish. That first time was the best ever.

With a raise of his left eyebrow, Steve suggested that I invite her to join us. I dictated a firm *nothing doing* to his shin with my right loafer and gave my full attention to the absorbing task of picking the label off my empty beer. Made no difference to Gloria. She turned up the voltage on her smile and asked Steve some dumb questions about sports.

I grabbed the chit and went to settle up even though it was Steve's round. He caught my signal and hustled over. We watched Gloria's lean back as she drifted toward the powder room. I wouldn't even say good-bye to her. I know

I could get her to leave me alone if I was nice to her. I just can't make myself do it.

I hailed us a cab and dove onto the cracked black vinyl seat. Safe.

"*Who* was *that?*" Steve gave a loud whistle. "Have you been holding out on me, my man?"

"My biggest fan. I told you about her. The wild thing who sent flowers to me at the station." I leaned forward and gave the cabbie block by block instructions for the most direct route to Steve's office.

"You see, pal," I gave it my best Bogey with a mouth full of marbles tone, "You see, sweetheart, it might be a bitch at the top of the heap, but there's always . . . consolations."

"And you've taken those consolations to heart, haven't you, Mr. Top Dog?"

"Yeah, I've been involved with a few femmes. So what. Not that one, man," I lied. "Not that psycho broad."

"What a waste! Tell me, aren't you ever tempted to overlook her intellectual deficits and make the most of her topography?"

"Give it up, meathead. You know as well as I that if I wasn't on the box every weeknight at six, she'd walk right by me. Life is tough in The Glory Zone. It was scary the way she started calling me up at the station after I did that piece on cocaine use in the NHL. That woman is pure trouble. She mailed me a pair of her lace panties with a note that said IMAGINE tucked inside. Nearly cost me my job, man."

"Must be tough for a guy like you who's trying to stay on the straight and narrow. Devoting every waking moment to making his marriage work."

"Right. We have a major investment there; can't have it slip-sliding away." No way, not while Angela has got the old vise grips on my balls. "That last promotion went right to her head. She's bringing in some major coin." I could never admit it to Steve, but the truth is, she's getting close to two hundred more than I do every cheque.

"It's a bitter pill, Mick. You never should have told Angela you were screwing around. A major tactical error. You tripped over your own dick."

"Yes. I beat my breast daily but Angela is scorched. Nothing makes a dint." For me, this is the worst. I'm losing the main event. To a girl.

"Do yourself a favour, stay single." I leaned forward and directed the driver to pull over in front of the supermarket at the next intersection. "You're better off without a wife. Trust me."

"Hey! Are you bailing? I thought you were headed down to the club for a workout."

"No way, amigo. Not under the new rules. I've got to buy a chicken and sling it in the oven. Angela is due back from the coast tonight and she expects a home-cooked meal. See how desperate I am?" I brandished my bandaged finger. "I've even taken up cooking."

"Come on, don't give me the kitchen sink routine. Grab something from a deli on the way home."

"No good. Then she'd bleat about that all night. Not acceptable under the new rules. I've got to *contribute something adult from my own time.* Anyway, I know I'm going to hear about my housekeeping. She always gripes when it's not up to her standards."

"Chin up, pal, you can go the distance." He landed a soft punch on my left biceps. "You're coming over to watch the fight with me Friday night. Right?"

"No question. Buddy'll be there." Doubt it, I said to

myself as the cab pulled away leaving me standing there with the rain seeping in through the leather soles of my Italian loafers. They'll be ruined before the bill comes through on my card. That's what I hate about life: you're always paying for the past in one way or another.

No question. That's what Angela said. There was absolutely no question of me going to watch the fights with my meathead friends. I'd be too busy helping my darling wife entertain her corporate clients at some Japanese restaurant where I'll pretend to love raw fish and sitting all night on a hard little cushion with my knees up around my ears.

No way I'd see Tyson take on Seldon. And live. My Angie does not like Iron Mike. It's a girl thing. 91, 93—these numbers mean nothing to her.

Ever notice how marital counseling comes right before martial arts in the Yellow Pages? Ange got really pissed when I pointed that out. She'd been screaming at me for an hour by then. Seems I forgot to close the dog out of the kitchen when I left the house. She got home before me and discovered that old Bowser had found a chicken carcass in the garbage and being the intelligent, resourceful type he is, hid it away for a rainy day. Are Labs not great dogs?

Trouble was he hid it in the new couch. Sliced open a down pillow and buried it deep. He must have been a real happy puppy until Angela waded toward him though the feathers. Screaming, ready to kill.

Marital therapy, martial arts. I was simply trying to lighten things up a little. It was Friday night and the fights were on at our house. Yeah. Bring on the raw fish!

So we started our weekly sessions with Dr. Geoff Barnes, Ph.D. The third man in our ring. The man who thinks my wife walks on water. "Try to match Angela's level of commitment to the marriage," he said to me over the tops of his glasses.

That's a tough one coming after Angela said right in front of him that she cannot remember what she saw in me in the first place. What a lie. She said she loved my brash energy. I know because I had to look it up. Do you believe that?

Truth is, she came on to me, asked to interview me for a paper she was writing on wrestling as theatre. Not my thing, I said. You must know the basics, she said. Told me I seemed dangerous to her. A hot little English major taking a walk on the wild side. I loved it. I impressed the hell out her by saying eppie-tome for e-pito-me. She thought it was sweet. I scored high. That round was *all* going my way.

Barnes is despicable—one of her favourite words for me—despicable 'cause I'm sure he uses his counseling sessions to troll for babes. I mean who wouldn't? I've caught him looking at her legs. And he saw me. He leaned back in his chair and began stroking his striped British school tie. It was the time we discussed how I almost got fired over the panties Gloria mailed to me at work.

"*Sic transit gloria mundi*," old Geoff said and then they laughed like a pair of real phonies. I thought it was another one of their riddles. I said you know I don't remember any French. I thought they were talking about someone named Gloria Mooney until they explained. The joke was on me. In Latin.

Gloria's last name is Bassett. That's one of the things I know about her. And she's divorced. She works as a manicurist somewhere down near the Royal York. She has great tits. She likes to drink cosmopolitans. It's not like she was a woman I would actually seriously date.

So later when we got home, I took Angela on again about it because I felt like she was cheating on me with Barnes even if she wasn't really. I said, you better be careful: some of those old teabags like it kinda kinky. Think about Prince Charlie. Don't act like I invented adultery.

I was really pissed with Dr. Barnes (call me Geoff) and told Angela I wasn't going back. I couldn't stand the way everything he said became her new gospel. I mean I could learn to talk in that fake New Age way if that's what it takes. But it's unnatural.

She really came down on me for being such an impossibly insensitive asshole when I asked her isn't it kind of funny that marital counselors are right next to martial arts in the Yellow Pages. I thought it was. I was taking her for granted. She considers that a big insult. I thought that was the point of marriage. That you got to take each other for granted. That you could count on being forgiven. For better or worse.

I said, "This is all you get. This is who I am."

"Is it National Cliché Week?" she yelled and locked herself in the bathroom.

"Shut up. Shut up," I yelled back.

Who knew how close love and hate can be? For sparring, for a domestic round, I prefer the Queensbury rules. Everything above the belt. The hot snap of leather on skin. The spray of sweat fanning out in the air as she reels from a crisp left jab. The sweet science of bruising.

Not that it matters now. That was our last big fight. I am f'ed. Facing a collage of doom. Ange and me, we're the worst match since Tyson and McNeely.

I went out to the Korean mom and pop's to get some smokes and found a foreclosure sign stapled to the door. It's a bitch how things change completely overnight. I guess they fell through a hole in the economy. I miss them already. I liked talking to the guy. Once we were talking about food and I happened to mention that I liked Korean food, which I guess I had a few times at the mall. He said he really liked Canadian food and when I asked what kind, he said, I like it all: McDonald's, Pizza Hut, Kentucky fried. I tried to tell him that wasn't the real thing. It's, you know, roast beef and gravy, turkey, mashed potatoes, apple pie, maple syrup. Ah, apple pie, he said, this I like. He always used to ask me about Angela. How's the missus? he'd say. Pretty lady, sir. You are a lucky guy, boy.

Now I won't have to tell him. Angie and I are through. There's a foreclosure sign on our love nest. It was over so fast I didn't get a chance to react. Like Spinks, from boxing icon to fistic mush in 91 seconds. I guess I was punching above my weight. Besides, anyone can disappoint you if you catch them at the wrong time. My problem is I have never really been alone. Since like high school.

She threw me out under a court order. Be out by noon on December 15, 1996. I couldn't get into my crappy new apartment until six o'fucking clock. So I drove around for the whole afternoon. Me and the dog. The car packed to the gills. Cruising. And all I thought of were her last words to me. We were standing on the porch and she had her hand out for my key. My key to my front door. She looked right at me and said "Now you know: Hell is the suffering of being unable to love."

That's from Dostoevski. He's an old favourite of Ange's with the crime and punishment stuff. I agree you gotta learn off your mistakes. I wanted to but the words made a mountain between us and I got left with sweet F.A.

Doctor Weltschmerz, I Presume

I HESITATED AT THE WATER'S EDGE. INSIDE THE *MIKVAH* THE air was warm and humid. From outside its steamy confines, I heard the melancholy voices of the members of the Beth Din.

"Why is she doing this?"

"Because she wants to suffer."

Three black-garbed figures stood at the door. Their backs to me. Three noisy crows flapping. I stepped down into the warm blue-tiled pool, abandoning the white sheet the babushkaed, Russian-speaking attendant had wound around me like a shroud.

I was setting off on a domestic journey. Of a different sort. I wanted to be like Mrs. Noah, sailing away with her husband and all the necessities and only their own children. Sam promised that we'd spend our fiftieth wedding anniversary on the moon. I couldn't wait that long. I knew our salvation rested in isolation.

"Is she in there yet?"

"We have to see her."

"Is she under the water?"

That Brezhnev-faced woman hiked up her skirts and waded in after me, gesturing for me to come toward her. She grabbed the sheet from the side of the bath and wound it tightly round me under the arms. She spun me around like a top until I felt a little dizzy. She roughly tucked the end of the sheet under my right armpit and clamped both arms down to my sides and hissed *stay, stay* at me through her stainless steel teeth. Silly goose, I thought. Send those men away. It is my husband who should see me taking the plunge. I eased my head under, eyes and mouth wide open.

The attendant called out to the rabbinic court.

"All right, she's under the water now," Rabbi Slonim said.

A torrent of Hebrew followed, prayers that circled back on themselves with comforting refrains. It was clear that I wasn't going to understand all that was said in my new land. Where thoughts were spoken in a new alphabet. An alphabet of woe.

I emerged from the *mikvah* with my new name, given to me by the rabbi. Not my choice but I may get used to it. I have another. Everyone should have a secret name.

Some believe that the essential character of a person is embodied in his name so that to know a name is to have power over that being and his fate. In such families, like my husband's, each person has two names—one for inside and one for outside the walls of the house. I am told this belief in the power of a name is behind the custom of not naming a newborn after a living person. For there could be confusion, an angel executing a decree of sickness might choose the wrong person for his unwelcome attentions.

Remember when Jacob wrestled all night with the angel? In the morning, Jacob asked his name. The clever angel would not tell in case Jacob tried to use his name in a magical spell.

Only the high priest may know the Name of the Lord. We do not even write it fully. Only the letters g-d are allowed. This, you know, is very different from Jesus, who is everyone's buddy. The friendly Son, not the distant Father or the Holy Ghost. Come to me, little children. Not that different from any other cult, Sam says. No different from the Hare Krishnas. They always befriend you first, then feed you crazy ideas later when you are in a weakened state.

It is dangerous if your name becomes too widely known. Ask Auntie Goldie. She knows of a woman who was in a terrible car crash possibly because of this. Auntie Goldie claims the husband, a cardiac surgeon, had to sit on a little stool beside the operating table and give instructions while the small-town doctor sewed his wife back together. Auntie Goldie says that after the woman got out of hospital, her family took her to synagogue for a special ceremony to change her name and keep away the evil eye. *Kaye ayn hore*, Auntie Goldie says and spits on the ground.

I studied long before choosing my name. Rachel and Leah were discarded for my Sam did not want anything to do with those two sisters. Not Rebecca either—too much trouble with the kids. Deborah or Devorah was a very modern girl. A prophet and military leader who sang of her victory. Devorah can translate as Dolly and I thought I'd like Sam to say Hello Dolly to me every morning.

The rabbi said you must take Ruth. For *my wife* and to remember who you are. I smiled and agreed that it is important to know who you are.

I have no attachment to my former, my real name. It's like a sheet of clear glass. I can look right through it at my New World. I want another, a secret name that only Sam would know. One that he cries out at the moment of climax. One he could use to call me to him from anywhere, the way, I've heard, a Mormon husband summons his wife to his side in the Celestial Kingdom by calling out her secret name told to him alone during their wedding ceremony.

I became a real *baleboste*, first-class homemaker. I bought in bulk, I cooked, I made my own fish. I ordered the help around. But for the sake of sanity, the line had to be drawn somewhere. Usually it's right across the kitchen, one half for *milchhik*, the other for *fleyshik*. *Parve* foods belong in the DMZ. I wanted to draw the line at a different place on the menu. I thought that at herring seemed to be a better place. I do not eat herring. I do not make any "mock" dishes. But if you need a recipe for mock *kishka* this is a good one I hear. A family heirloom, this recipe. Maybe you'll like.

MOCK *KISHKA*

2 stalks celery
2 medium onions, 2 carrots
(grind above in processor)
1 cup matza meal
1 cup cake meal
2 eggs
1 cup oil
$1/2$ tsp. pepper
1 tbsp. sugar
1 tsp. kosher chicken soup powder
(dissolved in 3 tbsp. boiling water)

Add the ground vegetables to above and mix well by hand. Smear two pieces of foil with oil. Make two rolls and place on foil. Wrap loosely and bake at 350 degrees for one hour. (Can be frozen.) When reheating, slice and put on fresh foil and heat at 350 degrees 'til hot. Serves 10.

THIS RECIPE WAS TUCKED INSIDE the nautilus shell we received from the rich cousin. "Sorry I am too busy to shop. I brought this back from my last trip. Your Sam always liked my *kishka* so I'm giving you the recipe. Remember satisfy your man in the kitchen and he'll satisfy you … you know where!"

Is there anywhere a complete list of foods permitted at Passover? Or maybe a complete list of those forbidden. (Of course, even I know ice cream is out. They had no freezers in the desert.) I'm just asking, you understand. Okay. What about a list of the 613 *Mitzvot*?

For *Shabat*, they say, always use white candles of good quality, non-drip, with a calm flame when burned in still air. Where is the air still? Not around my in-laws' table where my father-in-law, the retired button manufacturer, holds forth like King David. As soon as his wife Frima sets one bowl down on the table, he starts to eat. No matter what it is. Even if, for instance, it's potatoes, he takes a big serving and begins eating it up. He bellows for tea, which must be served in a glass. He has never drunk tea from a cup. And that's only one of the things he has never done. He's never polished his own shoes, sharpened a knife, never done laundry, never danced a waltz. He gives his list steadily, glaring at you with his dusty blue eyes. Frima accommodates his whims. His sharp tongue. Like a perfect magician's assistant, she is regularly sawed in half by it with no loss of composure or dignity.

Last week I dreamed that he was in bed with me, lying beside me, his head on my chest, his freckled, square-fingered hands stroking the globe of my belly, whispering "My world, my world."

Isolation. How I crave it. I want to be the country Sam lives in. I want a closed world like one of those plastic domes we had when we were kids. Not one with snowflakes though, don't want anything to remind me of gaudy old Christmas. No *gaudeamus igitur*.

Every day I scan the newspapers and journals for new jobs for him that are halfway across the continent, halfway around the world. I've slipped the ads into his briefcase, his pockets, rolled them up in his napkin, hoping that he'll find one when he is in a suggestible frame of mind. I follow the ad with articles about the climate, nearby golf courses, gourmet-dining spots. No luck so far, though I almost had him with San Diego and if he hadn't been so angry over the application I forged, we could be living there now. They were very interested in him there.

I am full of things I want. Every night I say a series of secret words. I've made my own list, for they say that certain words such as the *schema* are not to be used as magical incantations. I cannot help it. There's a tense, dark corner of Catholic in me still, squatting, waiting for a miracle, a blessing. Any sort of magic. Like when your husband enfolds you in his *talis* for the blessing of the *Kohenim* at the New Year, and for a time, you feel safe, well protected as Ruth did when Boaz spread his cloak over her.

Sam is seeing Dr. Berg, I see Dr. Berger and I guess that

means the kids will have to go to Dr. Bergest. I made that dumb joke at an all-shrink dinner party we hosted and after, Sam went ballistic. He does not agree that I have a future in stand-up comedy. Our guests were expecting a different kind of performance.

That girl is pure Id.

Isn't that a mean remark? Dr. Jonathan Weisskop said that about me right at the dinner table. He knew I was hurt. Did he think I wouldn't feel it? That it was happening to my clothes? Maybe I should wear gold lamé. It reminds me of armour. The golden armour of a Jewish princess. You really have to mind your mouth in a room full of psychiatrists. They watch, their ears prick up at some stray remark you make. And you can imagine they are taking notes for some questionable purpose that you won't find out about until later. What do women want, they laugh, larding their conversation with Freud's *bon mots*. And yes, even I know, sometimes a cigar is just a cigar.

What do women want?

I'm not telling.

I agree with Auntie Goldie. (And she's had lots of experience with shrinks.) They're like politicians, she says. *Me redt, me redt, un me shushkit nich.* They talk and they talk and they say nothing.

Of course, Sam is going to Dr. Berg five mornings a week because he needs to have an analysis as part of his training and a training analysis is analysis for a reason. Not for idle curiosity or neuroses like mine.

Or do I need analysis because I'm jealous of the attention Sam gets?

Am I?

That was Dr. Mel Green's interpretation. Let me tell you

it's not nice to be regarded as a minor disgrace. I've been judged and found wanting. I was afreud of that.

It was Sam's idea for me to go to Dr. Berger. He suggested it very gently and, of course, I cried. It's one thing to think you're going crazy but shouldn't other people pretend not to notice? I prefer the way Ricky Ricardo said it. "Lucy, you have to go to see a fiz a ciatrist." Except I can testify that there is no fizz in a psychiatrist.

There's more scythe. More cutting away. Call it psychic surgery, if you will. Hacking through the emotional jungle, the tangled web to the root of your troubles. Learning how inevitable it is that we lie to ourselves.

Sam's analysis has meant changes in our morning routines. A quickie if he's in the mood and then some tea. He no longer wants any conversation or breakfast. (How could I know he was eating it so my domestic urges would not be frustrated? As if I wanted to make oatmeal every day!) Nothing to interfere with his dream recall. He hides behind his cryptic crossword puzzle like a silent disapproving daddy and there are no cross words between us.

Dr. Berger's office is in the library of his lovely old house on St. Clair. Easy to get to from Moore Park. Behind his oak desk is a whole wall of bookshelves filled with impressively bound texts whose contents I imagine are stored as neatly in Dr. Berger's balding head. There is a beautiful rosy-hued Persian carpet on the bare floor. He sits on a tall grey velvet wing chair like the ones you see in the gentlemen's club scene in old British movies. He has a small round ottoman covered in a cross-stitch of jewel-coloured flowers. I think that Mrs. Berger made it. He likes to cross his neat little feet at the ankles, and that makes the tassels on his black loafers droop back against his argyle socks. It's only the socks and the bow tie that are different from session to session. The dark suits and starched white shirts all look the same. I'm glad that he is so much like Freud in this.

I am different each time. A little more pregnant, more or less confused or angry, more or less sure of what I know or know I want. I sit on the end of a cushy old black leather couch. I do not have to lie down but I may if I want to, he says.

In that room we talk about a miniature, a contained world. The world of my family, my life. I am trying to live an orderly life in a disorderly world. I believe I can control the laws of motion between Sam and me. Yes, I believe it, and my belief is based on my undoubted ability to control the world of this child while it is in my womb. I admit that only fifty per cent of its genes are mine. You can't fight Mother Nature but our baby is in my world now. For two hundred and eighty days we are one. That's not a simple matter. I asked Dr. Berger about this last week. I mean I asked him if our baby wasn't in analysis too. He smiled. That's as far as he'll go.

It is the doubling I like. The miniature world our babe lives in, inside me. When I converted I doubled myself. I became Ruth. Rabbi Slonim insisted on that name (because of Ruth from the Bible and because it is his wife's name). I do not mind. Here I am leading a double life among the alien corn.

Sam says he loves my body more now. He's proud of his little sperm's work. He snuggles up beside me with his ear to my belly, monitoring the swish of fluid, the kicks and jounces. He tells me all the medical words for what is happening but I don't pay the slightest attention. He loves to suck my nipples now and I encourage his loverly baby games so I'll be ready to nurse our son.

My Berger, or Dr. Weltschmerz, as I like to call him, because everyone needs a secret name and that seems to suit him—he's had all those years of listening to people's dreary secrets, lists of stupid cruelties, unattainable fantasies. He does not ask many questions. Like a mother, he accepts everything I offer. At each session I try something different to interest him. It's difficult to know what your doctor wants, what he needs. Pick any one of the dreams strung out along the backbone of the night.

In this room I am a double agent. I lie on a soft black leather couch and report to Dr. W. on my life, our lives. How much of what I say does he believe? What do I believe? He has already told me one valuable thing: that all memory has a degree of falsehood.

What does Sam tell Dr. Berg? If only I could think of a way to wire him for sound.

My teacher, Reb Seymour Walfish, told me many stories during our lessons. Did you know that in the seventeenth century, Elijah of Chelm created a *golem*, or robot of clay? He inscribed the name of g-d on its forehead and gave it life but withheld the power of speech. When his Frankenstein attained great size and strength, Elijah became frightened of its potential for destruction and tore the name of g-d from its forehead and it crumpled into dust.

Eleazer of Worms (now there's a name!) recorded the process and magical incantations to be recited over every stage in the making of a *golem*. Sometimes they used the word *emet* or truth on the forehead as an alternative to the name of g-d. The destruction of this creature was effected by erasing the first letter e in *emet* to leave *met* which means dead. By a simple reversal, the law of creation becomes the law of destruction.

When I put the word *emet* on the foreheads of my gingerbread men, Sam would not eat them though they are his favourite. Not until he broke off the heads and left them over. I saw he was worried about my power then. Before I was pregnant.

What will Dr. Weltschmerz make of this? I'm saving it for some dull session when I have no dreams to give him. When I need a lift in some deep way. Life is difficult. More or less so depending on your expectations. Did I really expect my husband to throw his *talis* across life's puddles for me?

And whom can you trust with your real worries? Mine include the crunch of hard boots on the bare floor outside my door. (Sam promises we will have carpet in the next house.) The children carried into the gas chamber. The piles of shoes, of eyeglasses.

Sam thinks I'm being deliberately difficult. Why don't you worry about the possible size of the kid's nose, he says. I understand that Sam doesn't want to hear about this when he gets home from the office. Like Dr. W., he has been listening the whole day. When he gets home, Sam wants a little snooze on the couch in his study followed by a three-course meal. Never leftovers.

Do you hear the rasp of my chains? Who said the chains of marriage are so heavy that it takes two to carry them? Sometimes three. Some French writer, I think. And we have four with our Berg and Berger.

Jonathan, Susan and Jesse Weisskop. Does that sound like a happy family? I thought it did. Jonathan, like Sam, a psychiatrist in training, also in analysis. Susan, like me, a convert, a mother. And Jesse a handsome bright boy like our son will be. They were, it seemed, only a few steps ahead of us.

Susan is my true friend. I refuse to speak of her in the past tense. She is bright and funny and kind. She's the only one I can joke around with about all this kosher stuff. We go out for cheeseburgers with bacon and she'll say to the waiter—"make sure that the bacon is crisp for my friend Mrs. Strimel." We make lunch reservations under our fake matronly names. She's Mrs. Rose Tzitzit and I'm Mrs. Faye Strimel.

Later, when unhappy differences arose and the Weisskops broke up, she turned her back on all of this. She said, "I've had a lot of Jewish men but now I've had it with Jewish men. Neurotic, clingy mama's boys. Not a *mensch* among them. They think they want chocolate mousse, but give them a taste and they want to go straight back to rice pudding."

After the separation, her father got sick and she went up to Montreal to be with him. Jonathan moved back into the house to look after Jesse. When she returned, Jonathan refused to leave. He went underground, living in the base-ment bedroom. Like a mole he lived—creeping around, answering the phone, pretending to take messages, paying the rent on his empty apartment.

I said she should put his things out on the lawn and change the locks. Sam disagreed. Susan agreed with him. She would never subject Jonathan to that humiliation. She was trying words. Words were their only weapons. He never laid a hand on her. Love loses its energy, she said. Everyone knows that. It's no one's fault. And Dr. W. explained that you see there is only one awful thing in this world. And that is that everyone has his reasons.

I'll never understand how he managed to live like that. I swear he became hairier, paler, hunchbacked, living underground. Weisskop seems to have a talent, maybe even a passion for unhappiness. For over seven months he never once spoke to Susan. Only Jesse. She told me the whole story at lunch and when I asked how she could stand it, she said she forgave him. She also said she was afraid of his quiet hard centre.

Withholding forgiveness is an act that isolates, according to Dr W. Can you tell me—is pure sorrow more possible than pure joy? I think it is certainly more likely.

One week after our last lunch she was dead. A drunk driver came over the median at her car on the QEW. I stood beside my friend's dark open grave wondering, Who knew Susan's name? What angel of darkness confused her with someone else named Sarah? I felt queasy and a little frightened at the sight of that gloomy rectangle. I had to step back. My belly sometimes makes me a little tipsy.

I did not want to see Dr. W. after Susan's funeral. I am travelling alone now in a foreign land. No one speaks my tongue. I can only think straight in one language. If only I could speak the language of angels.

I have been told that I will never know what Israel means. That's true. I know it only as a place of remembered beauty. Everybody knows that boat is leaking. I cannot take on these alien griefs that have seeped down, staining the centuries. It seems so useless. Don't ask me for that. Not now. I know now that all I need is a map. Some hope of safe passage under the glare of distant stars.

I want to be like Mrs. Noah with a brilliant crown of silver hair, standing beside my husband at the helm. Watching for the dove to return with an olive branch in its beak. Looking out for the distant shores of blessing. A further horizon, where we may find a Garden of Eden. I don't want to be left outside of Eden. I want to pitch my tent under the Tree of Life, for they say that all its ways are ways of pleasantness and all its paths are Peace.

There wasn't anything I could say to Dr. W. about Jonathan and especially not about Susan. All I had to offer was a dream I had the night before she died. I wanted to see what Dr. W. would make of it.

In my dream, my sons and I were preparing to leave after spending the weekend at a wonderful country house. I went upstairs to collect our things. A plump ancient lady called out to me that we were welcome to extend our stay. The rooms were high ceilinged, airy and bright with jewel-toned silk oriental carpets on polished floors. I went from room to room looking for our things. In one room I found Leonard Cohen sleeping on a chaise lounge under a window. Outside all was misty green. Lombardy poplars marched across the lawn. There was a table at the foot of the couch; on it sat a wooden box with many small compartments lined with green felt. I looked over at Leonard and he woke.

"I'm sorry," I said. "I didn't mean to disturb you." He smiled.

"I thought you might be able to use these." I looked at my open palm and saw two smallish wood screws painted black and one fine nail. I put them into one of the sections of the flat wooden box.

Dr. W. was cross with me. I think. Very slowly, like I was an idiot child, he asked, "And what then is a *kohen*? Do you remember? Were you offering salvation to a priest? Who in your family has a priest-like role? Who hears confessions?"

How do I know? The subconscious is like a magician. If

only it would work regular hours. And file more comprehensive reports.

I swore then that I was through with it. I'm all talked out of the talking cure. This rigorous sifting through the dank midden of my psyche. This dumb exercise. Like Nick Caraway, I want the whole world to be standing at moral attention for the rest of time. I have nothing to say to Sam. We interpret things differently now. I no longer feel as close to him. Do I go through the motions until the feelings return, like Dr. W. says? Okay, there'll be a chicken on the table every Friday night. Believe me, I can serve chicken five hundred ways. That should be enough time.

On my way to the next session, a huge man from Jamaica got on the streetcar and sat down beside me. He was hauling a battered fake leather suitcase. A blinding yellow sticker on its side advised RELAX GOD IS IN CHARGE. Underneath, in smaller letters it said *Faith Restoration Centre* but there was no address.

He tilted his head and smiled at me. "What's your trouble, sister?" he asked. Without waiting for a reply, he reached over to lay his broad pink palm like a poultice on my forehead. "Dear Lord," he prayed, "please give this child the strength she need to carry on." He left his hand there for about a whole minute and I felt that energy burning its way into my brain. Like a switch was thrown and the flow of all those multi-syllabled chemicals was stopped. Altered.

I jumped up and got off at the next stop, Avenue Road and St. Clair. I sat in the Second Cup coffee place for three hours thinking it all over, waiting for a further sign. I realized that I can't go out in public now and Sam is not going to talk me out of it. My thoughts kept doubling back to that five minutes of the day when I wanted to lean over the breakfast table and say I've fallen in love with Dr. W. He's my perfect hero now.

Going out is too risky while I'm pregnant. I'm going to stay inside until I know the name of the muddy-footed little angel who's got to come down and look after me.

I gave most of the money for my session to the squeegee kids and took a cab home. That girl with the blue hair looked hungry. Sam found me in bed with a box of tissues. He was sweet about it all. That's my Sam. He's what I live for—the steady beat of his heart.

"I don't want anything bad to happen to us," I said.

"It won't. It won't," he whispered as he kissed my belly.

"But," I said, "do you really believe that?"

May 22, 1954

UNDER THE HOT DAPPLING SHADE OF THE NORWAY MAPLE Elizabeth Doyle lay in wait for Frau Schumacher. As she waited, she played pretend skipping. Over and over she sang:

> *Teddy Bear, Teddy Bear, turn around round round*
> *Teddy Bear, Teddy Bear*
> *Touch the ground, ground, ground.*

She skipped until her legs grew weary. Then she embraced the bus stop pole and began to shinny up its smooth cream surface. She wanted to get past the blue band so she could claim at recess that she had gotten "bluesies." Most of the big boys from the neighbourhood were up on the Crescent. Elizabeth could hear them calling their war orders back and forth between the elms. They were putting booby traps made out of ladyfingers into the rough bark of the elms to see who could give the best scare. The acrid smell of the fireworks made her uneasy. Her hands began to slip and she said *Black Sambo, Black Mumbo, Black Jumbo* to herself very quickly, but it didn't work. She eased herself to the ground. Her dada said that magic words were very sly. She didn't always get them right.

The bus lumbered down the block and hissed to a stop. Its black rubber-gasketed doors folded back to disgorge a very warm loaf of a woman. Alva Schumacher. She was plump all over like Mrs. Claus, with her white hair braided and coiled at the nape and covered with a fine cobweb net. She held her market basket a little away from her body as she descended to the sidewalk, intent on the placement of her stout black oxfords.

"So. You make me a welcome party, Elisabett," said Frau Schumacher. "This is so nice. *Ach*. It is hot, isn't it, *liebchen*? Will you come and take a glass of lemonade on the porch with me now? My poor old feet want me to sit down."

This was exactly what Elizabeth had been waiting for. She slipped her hand into her friend's. They crossed the street, kitty-corner, and continued past Elizabeth's house, their steps matching easily.

Nora Doyle scarcely noticed the tags of their soft-voiced talk floating up through her open bedroom window. She lay transfixed on the knobby top of her white chenille bedspread, caught in some limbo between sleep and waking. She'd peeled off her girdle and stockings and tossed them on top of the navy linen suit that she'd left crumpled up on the armchair. An ice pack was cooling out her screeching headache and she began to wish that Tim were there to rub her feet. Tim certainly knew feet. *They are my bread and butter*, he'd say with a laugh and then pinch his nose. His children did not go barefoot. Nora, Elizabeth, and the lads always had the best in his store. She looked down over her flowered duster at her neat white feet pointing to the ceiling, then at the green walls surrounding her. She thought of how strangely they seemed to flatten out and become the sea she and Tim rode at nights, wrestling with their natures on the dark wooden bed.

They thought they were so clever, the pair of them. They'd seen no future on the farm. It isn't a thing you can do, unless you purely love it. On this they agreed. It was lucky for them too, that Tim's sister, Ellen, was willing to have their mother come to live in with her family. The old place was sold off and the money divided.

Despite the post-war housing shortage, they found a sweet red brick nest on a street where their neighbours were cozied up like brooding hens. Nora was pleased they were not the over-friendly type. She enjoyed a pleasant conversation, now and again; who doesn't? But you wouldn't want to be always having ladies in for coffee and the like. A person would not be getting her work done. Nora preferred to get things done up early, and leave some time in the evenings for the family.

Elizabeth knew all the neighbours, though. Our little ambassador, Tim called her; he would let her get away with sweet murder, he would. He let her stop taking an afternoon rest to keep away the polio before she even started into grade one. Easy enough for him to do. He didn't have to listen to the other mothers raving away about being safe, not sorry. He said she was every bit as sweet and pretty as that Shirley Temple. And she could sing just as well, to boot. The apple of his eye, she was. He was not the one to nurse the children when they were ill or comfort them when nightmares came. Their breadwinner would turn his broad warm back and get his sleep then. *You don't have to listen to those old cows,* he often told her. But there were ways of getting entangled with the neighbours he didn't know about. This morning's episode had begun last Sunday, on the way out from ten o'clock High Mass, when that old cat, Mrs. Michael Henley, had the gall to point out that Elizabeth's blue Swiss dot from last year was looking too small on her. *You'll have to put a stone on top of her head* was what she said. It was true; the waist was inching up toward the child's rib cage. So, today, as soon as Tim and the boys had gone off fishing, Nora gave Elizabeth a scrubbing and they set off for the shops.

On the second floor of Kruger's department store, they sat regally on the sweaty leather seats of oak armchairs while the clerk, Frieda Schmidt, pawed her way through the rack of party dresses. Her broken nails with their chipped red polish irked Nora unreasonably. Even more than the darkening circles that spread out under the sleeves of her blue nylon blouse. A *dummkopf* who hadn't even the sense to wear cotton in this heat. And such an odour. Glory! What could she know about clothes? If it were up to me, thought Nora, the woman would be given her notice on the spot. As Tim would say, she was not up to snuff. You have to give the public what they want or they'll take their business elsewhere. He'd probably laugh and say Frieda Schmidt's trouble was that she had eaten one dumpling too many. She looked slovenly to Nora, standing there with no foundation garment on. Belly hanging out like she was five months gone. She reminded Nora of a codfish with those big pale lips gone slack. All she did was hold the dresses out stiff on their hangers. Left Nora to do the entire fitting herself.

Frieda was oblivious to her customers. She felt a small flutter in her belly, the straps of her sandals biting into her swollen feet. She moved sluggishly in the thick fog that isolated her from all of life. Shamed. The business of little girls' dresses was completely beyond her. Her fingers stumbled with the wrapping of the parcel under the mother's impatient eyes.

Frieda took the bill and money and folded the two together and placed them in a small cylinder of brass-coloured metal. The cylinder's brown felt padded ends were given a deft twist, inserted in the air pipe and carried off with a great hissing suck from the vacuum.

Dada had told Elizabeth that leprechauns operated this marvelous machinery and directed traffic in the tubes. She wished to see if they looked like the people in her books about Noddy and his friends. She was silently counting off the seconds the journey took when her calculations were interrupted by a thought that seemed to spring from the darkness of the tubes.

"Momma, what's a refugee? Wanda Kosinski says she's a refugee from a concentrated camp. She said she was born there."

Frieda's brassy head jerked back as nausea heaved an acid wave up the back of her throat and she bit down hard on her own clammy hand.

The metal cylinder had dropped out of its magic door as the last word left Elizabeth's mouth and its arrival absorbed her. When she looked up for an answer, both grown-ups seemed frozen, as if by a wicked fairy's wand. She blinked hard twice to break the spell.

Nora reacted first. She jumped up and snatched the paper carry-handle out of Frieda's hands. She knew

Elizabeth was talking about the d.p. camp over beside the wartime armories. You simply could not keep a thing from that child with her rambling all over the neighbourhood. And all with her father's blessing, if you please.

Frieda stood silently, her hands restlessly smoothing the skirt over her pot of a belly.

"Elizabeth," croaked Nora, "we will talk about that when we are at home." Clearly the subject was not fit for polite conversation, like frogs' insides, men's things and farting at the dinner table.

The Doyles made their way in silence down the wide oak staircase with the cleats on Elizabeth's shoes echoing the muffled tap of Nora's heels. In unison, they passed by bolts of summer-coloured fabric, rows of trimmings and laces and legions of buttons on review. Nora swooshed them out through the revolving door, halting abruptly in the white-hot morning. She braced herself, moving her right foot out a few inches, and breathed deeply. She could almost taste the water in the air. Nora looked south, down the main street. No trolley in sight. Carefully sucking her lips inward, she blotted her forehead and upper lip with a lace-edged show hankie.

"We must have just missed it," she sighed, as she absently settled her straw clutch purse under her arm and put out her hand to meet Elizabeth's. Nora hadn't a clue of what she should say. The child could see this and acknowledged it by giving a little squeeze to the gloved hand encircling her own. She was rewarded with one of her mama's wide smiles. Elizabeth already knew when not to press for an answer. There were some you could have when the time was right, or when you were old enough to understand. She knew to watch and wait. Hand in hand, they crossed the street and entered Woolworth's, where Nora bought an ice cream sandwich made with fresh waffles for Elizabeth. They walked up to the trolley stop in front of the old red brick hotel and sat on the park bench outside its brass plated door. Nora and Tim had gone through that same door on the evening of their wedding day. They had eaten the first breakfast of their married life in the stately dining room with its polished oak and gleaming silver. The waiter had startled her, she remembered, by pulling out her chair. She had confessed to Tim that it did seem a bit bold, having breakfast with a man who wasn't her old pa, but she hoped to accustom herself to it in the near future. He'd laughed softly and taken her hand across the table. This memory soothed Nora and, buoyed by its phantom embrace, she reached out to tuck her daughter's curls behind the perfect small ears with care both fierce and tender.

Wartime didn't touch my life hardly at all, she thought. We did lose Uncle Dave's Joe at Dunkirk and that was a sad death for his family or maybe a blessing in disguise, what with the way he was taking to the whiskey on his last leave home. Joe was drunk as a lord when they carried him on to the train at Stratford with his sisters crying all around him. Aunt Eileen always kept his picture and his medals set up on a doily on top of the piano in the front room as a little shrine. She would not hear a hard word against him or any of the others, who became regulars at the Legion after. Most of the families had sent one or two lads; being the flat-footed only son of a widow with a dairy farm had spared Tim Doyle. Of course we had rationing same as in the city, only it was harder for them. Well, who's going to starve when there are cattle standing there and chickens running in the yard? If you needed more butter, you just churned up some. That's when we stopped putting sugar in our tea though; it was the tea and sugar we missed mostly. And the gas. The government began putting a kind of purple dye into the gas you were to use for the farm machinery. It'd stain your motor if you were to use it in the car. Tim was friendly with the agent over on his line so the fella would hand him the package of powder and say *I ain't looking*. That's how Tim got enough to take me home from the odd social. We were always grateful to the government man for that. For our wedding, I wore a plain suit and the wedding cake was mostly raisins but you couldn't call that a hardship.

When Kruger's closed its doors for the week, Frieda slogged homeward through thick currents of heat that radiated up from the pavement. She was in no hurry to see her father so soon after the quarrel they had had the evening before. That evening had been unseasonably warm too and Frieda had returned to find her widowed father, home from his job at the rubber factory, already seated and eating at the kitchen table. Gerhardt Schmidt was dining on sausage and eggs with sauerkraut all washed down with cold ale. There were beads of sweat rolling down his forehead and the sides of his stein. When the smell of his meal got the best of her and she began to heave, Gerhardt had reached over and delicately tapped the swell of his daughter's belly with the tip of the butcher knife.

"Fräulein, was ist das, der Lebensborn, vielleicht?"

Frieda made no reply to his cold eyes. She went to her room. She stayed there, on the bed, sleeping, or silent until morning. Some of the time was given over to long, imagined conversations with her dead mother. She explained all she could about Ernst. Told her mother again how they met. How she and Irma Hahn spent their Saturday evenings at a small table at the back of the German club. Most Saturdays, Frieda just sat, slowly sipping her way through the three drinks of vodka and orange juice she enjoyed each week. With each drink the pink in her cheeks deepened. When the band would start up with a polka, Irma might, if she wasn't with a favourite partner, excuse herself and come over to pull Frieda onto the floor for a few spins. The hectic rhythms danced the two women into a state of giddiness that sparkled in their eyes and shimmered on their skin. Thus was she beautified, this lumpen *fräulein*. Her rare flowering proved an irresistible enticement for Ernst Rumpel. It was Frieda's hard luck that the first man she attracted was a horn player addicted to making women glow for him. She was able to enjoy the magic of being loved for seven and one-half months before the unwelcome news of her pregnancy smothered their romance.

Shame became her constant companion. It stole her strength like a charm. It went deep. Deeper than the wartime humiliation of trying to make her dry mouth spit out her German name to claim the ration coupons.

When Frieda crawled in that hot May evening from Kruger's, Gerhardt had already gone out to his Saturday session of Solo, conversation and beer. She lay down fully clothed and slept deeply for several hours. The air was overripe with humidity. A thunderbolt jarred her from her dreams. The only image that stayed with her was the face of a small boy, standing in front of a pile of rubble. Blond, handsome, blue eyed. He looked a little like Ernst. The same dimpled smile. Ernst. He would be at the club tonight. Frieda hurried to change to her pink halter-top dress. Ernst always liked her in pink. She slipped on her white bolero sweater and bolted out into the warm rain, leaving the house ablaze with light.

The drummer was first to see Frieda stumble into the club, wild-eyed and dripping. He leaned over and prodded Ernst with his drum stick. At the end of the number, Ernst slipped off the bandstand and approached his bedraggled mistress.

"*Kleiner Schatz*, you surprise me. I said I would call you. Look, we cannot talk here. Come, we go out to *mein* car and get ourselves a little bit privacy." He took her by the elbow and squeezed gently.

Frieda measured his smile against the edge in his voice and followed him across the gravel to his new sky-blue Chev. He held her hand and talked in even tones about someone he knew who knew someone else who knew a woman she could go to for help with her little problem. He spoke softly in German, pleased to see her slowly calming.

"Wait here, the night is almost out. I'll take you home. Listen to the radio for a while. Sleep a little, *liebchen*."

Frieda sat there numb and obedient until the rain stopped. Then suddenly she hitched herself over to the driver's side and turned the key in the ignition. She drove with deliberate care through the rain-soaked city on a familiar route that led to the river flats where she and Ernst often held their rendezvous. She stopped at the T intersection in front of the old country hotel by the bridge. Breathing heavily, almost sobbing aloud, she turned the wheel and drove the brand new car down the embankment and into the swollen river. As the dark waters rushed in through the open windows, Frieda began to whimper softly. She let go of the wheel. Mama. Mama, she called, the river is cool. I swim to you. She gripped the top of the steering wheel hard and pulled her body up from the seat. She gasped as she bumped her head on the padded grey baize of the ceiling. She sat down. The water rose quickly, chilling her rib cage. It crept up to cover her bare shoulders. Mama! She saw her mother look up from her mending and open her arms. She smiled. The last image Frieda had was of that blond dream boy.

At that same moment, Elizabeth was sleeping soundly under the Sandman's umbrella. Her sleep, the sleep of an innocent child, the sleep that refreshes like no other, was not disturbed by that evening's electrical storm. She'd remembered, as she was drifting off, that mama had not had that little talk with her when they returned from their shopping trip. That meant she would not be hearing of it again. Elizabeth was glad of that.

None of the pieces of the puzzle fit together but they all passed before her eyes as she lay sucking on her rag doll's hand. Elizabeth had been drawn to Wanda by the Polish girl's strange speech. Elizabeth had never imagined that a girl, who was the same age as herself, but seemed older, would turn up with only two dark dresses to her name and such an odd way of speaking. Did she have special powers like Pippi Longstocking? Elizabeth volunteered to walk home with Wanda that first day, eager to see where she lived. Wanda led her down the street past the army camp and around to the chain link enclosure that stood next to it. The buildings within the enclosure looked more like sheds than real houses. Or maybe house skeletons. No one had bothered to put bricks over the tarpaper. There weren't any sidewalks either. Right in front of the house that turned out to be Wanda's was an open drainage ditch that they crossed by means of a sagging wooden plank.

Elizabeth could tell that Wanda's mother was not pleased to see a guest in the house. She didn't look up from the potatoes she was peeling with a sharp-looking knife. She might be a pretty lady but you couldn't tell, she seemed so unhappy. Her hair was all tucked up under a big kerchief like what the Queen wears to ride her horses. Elizabeth guessed it was because of the chill in the house. Quite a few sentences were exchanged in a queer-sounding lingo.

Wanda crossed the speckled linoleum and put her books down next to the pile of potato skins. Elizabeth couldn't make out if Mrs. Kosinski was angry or if maybe she was getting another baby. Some mothers got quiet and tired like this when they were having another child. She never found out, though, because Wanda turned to her and said, "I walk you now to the gate and good-bye."

The two girls confined their friendship to school hours after that day, sharing their imperfect knowledge of the world around them. Elizabeth did not believe in all of Wanda's old life across the ocean where there were supposed to be real castles, lots of soldiers and ovens that people got burned up in. Anyone knows you can do that to a wicked witch but not a real person. She decided that Wanda must be mixed up. Her English was not too good. And where Wanda had lived. It must be a camp for thinking. Concentrate, concentrate, was what the Sisters were always telling the Grade Eights to do in arithmetic lessons.

Elizabeth had thought of asking Frau Schumacher about all of this while they sat together behind the cool shelter of the trumpet vine. Then she remembered how frightened she had been when she found out the Earth was a planet. Alva's quick fingers were busy twisting the crochet cotton into delicate lace pineapples that would grow to cover the high polish of her dining room table in tropical profusion. Elizabeth wondered if Frau Schumacher missed her dead husband, Karl. She didn't miss him at all. He had always frightened her a little. His huge butcher's hands and his oompah voice.

Dada called him Old Dunderbeck. Whenever the Schumachers were mentioned, he'd throw back his head and recite:

> Old Dunderbeck, old Dunderbeck
> How could you be so mean?
> To ever have invented such a horrible machine?
> Poor pussy cats and long-tailed rats
> They'll never more be seen
> For they've all been ground to sausages
> In Dunderbeck's machine.

With Herr Schumacher resting for a whole year under the green grass of the old Lutheran cemetery, Elizabeth's visits to Alva's became more frequent. She liked to be asked into the bright white and yellow kitchen to help tend the two canaries, Elise and Franz, or to wind thick skeins of wool into smooth balls. For her birthday, Frau Schumacher had given Elizabeth a fine lawn hankie with mountain flowers embroidered on the corner. But the best gifts were her stories. She would tell about Rumpelstiltskin, Hansel and Gretel or Elizabeth's favourite, "The Boy and the Lion." That was the story that Frau Schumacher offered on that warm afternoon.

"Once upon a long ago time, there was a sleepy town that lived at the edge of a great plain with a big big mountain at its back. A Beast troubled this town. A very wild Lion who came down to prowl by the gates. *Ja.* Everyone, the mothers, the fathers and the children, they were quaking in their very boots at the sound of his such great roaring. All they could think of was the tearing teeth he had. He was so fierce that no man could look him in the face. These villagers thought of so many plans what to do for driving him away.

"The oldt fathers of the town thought maybe he is chust a little bit hungry. So they got a fresh sweet lamb killed and threw it down to him. That too smart Lion, he gnawed it down to the bones with smacking his big lips and shaking his golden curly head. He took from it all what he wanted and padded away. The villagers were so happy to see his tail disappear into the dark forest.

"But next evening, for sure, when those stars begin peeking out, back he comes to prowl around der walls again, roaring and strutting like he knows he is King of der Wilds. Families what were sitting eating the supper und small ones playing by the hearth. All began to tremble at his fine roaring and the food would no more go down der throats. Babies stuck to mama's skirts and all the dogs started out with loudish barking. That night those villagers climbed up on the walls and down a net dropped over the Lion. *Ach,* they slept strong that night. They didn't know that Herr Lion was chewing his way out from their thick ropes like it was noodles. And he crept away.

"On der third night, those villagers got themselves with another plan. They sent up to the bell tower, the best hunters all with the bow and arrows. Der arrows fell on him like rain. Not one touched a hair of him. De oldt fathers were run out of tricks how to get rid of Herr Lion. They started arguing mit themselves. No one got an idea to hope from.

"Now there was in the town an orphan mit a so sweet voice. This boy, he bravely entered the council chambers where the town fathers sat scratching in their beards. He went up to the one with the longest and pulled on the sleeve of him. The boy whispered his offer to sing for the Lion. The old men were doubting and some said it was foolish idea. After much talking, they agreed to give the try to the boy. Some thought but none said it would not be much loss if the boy did not make success, as he had no one to mourn him. That evening, when the sun set, the boy, dressed in a long white robe, stood tall as he could in front of the gate. Everyone trembled as the Lion began prowling the night. The boy took a deep deep breath and, as the gates were rolled back, began to sing an angel song. So tender was his music, the Beast came to lie at his feet and let the boy caress his noble head."

Alva was pleased when she saw how her tale enchanted her little guest. The arbour at the back of her garden was covered in myrtle rooted from her wedding bouquet. Though it had flourished, as had her marriage to her dear Karl, they had not been blessed with a child. So, never having a cub of her own to lick into shape, Alva took to borrowing other people's daughters.

Nora did not begrudge the time her daughter spent with Frau Schumacher. She thought they made a strange pair and wondered to Tim what they might find to talk about. Elizabeth never let on. Likely she badgered the old woman, as she did every one, with her outlandish questions. Last week Elizabeth had wanted to know how long the world's life would be. As if there was an answer. Not even the Holy Father in Rome could keep up with her.

They didn't seem so foreign, the Schumachers. Not when

she remembered the first Germans she met at the high school up home. Mother warned her off that lot of square-heads, mostly because they were Protestants. They were uncouth too, and never did learn to speak the language right. It made the old girl savage, it did, if she were to hear them tack an "*ach*" or a "once already yet" on the tail of a sentence. But you couldn't blame the German people, or, at least, not the ones who were here all along, for the sorry shape of the world these days. You couldn't put it on to anyone in particular, now could you?

A vague uneasiness clouded Nora's heart that afternoon, as she sat perched on the kitchen stool, chipping away at the accumulated ice in the fridgidaire. She longed for a perfect answer to lighten the burden of Elizabeth's questions. Love thy neighbour as thyself, she thought. Or maybe, you reap what you sow. She weighed every gem of wisdom she possessed. All were wanting and clanged in her ears like hollow ignorant lies.

This Bitter Earth

"Water was running the whole night. It's the same thing." Eva shrugged.

I took out my hankie, swiped my forehead and dabbed away at my hairline, moustache and chin. After the hike up to the third floor, I was *shvitzing* like Satchmo. My sister gave a weary sigh. We were standing in the hallway outside a dark, heavily varnished oak door, waiting for Ada Dorfman to answer our knock.

"She crawls as slowly as a beetle."

"This is the most depressing block in the entire North End and I've been in them all." I put my left hand on the beige-painted cinder block wall next to the doorframe and leaned forward to rest my forehead beside my hand. The wall was cool. I felt like I was at the Western Wall about to *daven.*

"And this carpet; it's so ugly, you could weep."

It had an abstract design of bright yellow and orange on dark brown overlaid with geometric shapes in black. "I remember this product. It was on sale in Stalingrad in 1953. Five rubles a metre."

"Enough with the smart talk, mister. She's coming."

"Coming," I snorted, "she isn't even breathing hard."

Eva gave me a sharp elbow in the ribs.

"What are we doing here?" I whispered.

Ada's black eye filled the peephole in the door. She kept us under inspection on the door mat while she fiddled with the bolts on her door.

"They took it away," she said. "The soldiers came for the baby in the lobby."

While we stood on the threshold, Ada began to sing in a monotone:

> *Ikh hob a kleynes yingle,*
> *A zimele gor fayn:*
> *Ven ikh derze im, dakht zikh mir,*
> *Di gantse velt is meyn*

Eva and I each took hold of an elbow and swiveled her around in the doorway and walked her into the foyer as if she were a little kid. She made no effort to resist us but continued to sing:

> *Nor zeltn, zeltn ze ikh im,*
> *Mayn sheyem, ven er vakht:*
> *Ikh tref in shtendik shlofndik,*
> *Ikh ze im nor bay nakht.*

She always sings that little song about the sleeping baby when she gets winged out. Life has let her down hard.

I knew it, I said to myself. I knew what we would find when the door opened. A crazy woman dressed in her dead husband's suit, her grey hair in a brush cut, her pockets stuffed with heels of rye bread. Ada used to be stout. Blown up with sour cream and *schmaltz* so she'd barely fit into one of those flowered cotton housedresses she wore. Now she had lost half her weight and her skin coarsened. She looked like a balloon collapsing with a slow leak.

Ada's suite is furnished with a French provincial-style couch upholstered in powder blue brocade, a fruitwood end table and on that, a porcelain shepherdess holding a clock and with a fancy pleated lamp shade of yellowed silk growing out of her head. That lamp looks like it once belonged to Marie Antoinette. There's a lousy seascape on the wall, strictly paint by the numbers, like a giant postcard. Behind a folding screen is a single bed with a white vinyl headboard and a second end table. Dozens of *yartzheit* candles. Some burnt out and others still burning cover its surface.

For my husband, she said when Eva asked whose *yartzheit*.

"Why so many?" asked Eva.

"One for every year we had together."

Okay, so that's not right, but what do you expect?

In the kitchenette a card table covered with a blue and white plastic cloth, and two folding chairs complete the furnishings. Everything just as it was when her stepsons moved her in one week after their father's funeral. She doesn't need much, they say, she's in the hospital for three or four months of the year. They pay the rent and she lives on who knows what. Bread and salt and all that's in the fridge—one wilted cabbage. *Banyak.* Neither Sid nor Jack lives here now. They stay far away in Montreal. Gerry stayed in Winnipeg but he didn't mix in.

Then Eva told me to check the closets.

"For what?" I asked.

"Just look," she said.

I called out the inventory from the front hall: "One beige raincoat, one pair black winter boots, one grey toque, one tweed overcoat, four pails water."

"That's enough," she hollered.

"Enough what?" I asked.

"Enough *kipitok*, enough boiled water. I'm calling for the doctor."

Eva coaxed Ada over to sit on the side of the bed. Then she took a kitchen towel, folded it, and handed it to her as if it were an infant.

This trick fools Ada every time. She thinks she is holding the baby she lost during the war. In the camp. She never saw that one. I guess that's why she can believe the baby that was left behind in the apartment lobby was hers. And because the police took it away. That was more than two years ago, but for her everything is like yesterday.

"Little dove, my little dove," Ada crooned to her cloth bundle, smiling her china smile. She can spend much of her day like that with her face buried in death's dark shoulder, smelling the mud, hair, and water.

I went and sat down in the kitchen. Exactly where we were sitting. At that card table. When Eva gave her the news only two weeks ago.

"Ada, what can I tell you? I don't want it should be me to tell you. But you have to know. I was there and I must speak. Ada, please sit down. Such news you don't want to take standing."

There were only two chairs so I got up and leaned against the counter like an eavesdropper while Eva gave out the bad news.

"Ada," Eva took her hand and sandwiched it between hers. "Ada, are you listening? They buried your Gerry, your little Gershon yesterday. As G-d is my witness. It's killing me to say this. It's a knife in the heart. He's in the Hebrew Sick cemetery and there was no *shiva*. I said *Kaddish* for you. So did Murray and Bella Katz. I heard about it by accident only at the last minute. He got a cancer and it was quick." Eva warned me before she wouldn't say AIDS but cancer instead of. Ada doesn't know the difference. "They were all there. I mean Sid and Beryl, Jack and Ruth, Gittel and Freddie, Dora and David, even the children."

I thought of saying don't leave out Gerry's little *faigle*. 'Cause Frankie was there, all bundled up in his mother's black mink. His performance was the highlight of the whole funeral. It was a graveside service, so we huddled like cows around the bright green plastic carpeting that framed the grave. After they lowered the coffin and Rabbi Schnier led the *Kaddish*, people came forward to take a handful of the frozen earth to throw down on the coffin. When it was Frankie's turn, he pelted down his handful first. Then he picked up the gravedigger's shovel and began madly filling in the hole and wailing and crying out loud. Sid and Jack had to strong-arm him to get the shovel and drag him away. They put him in Murray and Bella's car and they got stuck with driving him home. He's still living in Gerry's condo on Wellington.

Ada sat there like a stone the whole time until Eva stopped talking.

That's when I heard it for the first time. The way some

one who is really *meshuga* talks. She looked at Eva and said, "I was born on the Sun. I was very beautiful. My curls were made of real gold. My mother was jealous of me so she sent me here to live. There is no water on the Sun."

Then she covered her eyes with the palms of her hands and said softly, "I wish for a piece of bone from my son so I can have some peace."

Eva looked over at me and rolled her eyes. She doesn't get it, her eyes said.

Today, after the ambulance left, we went to Eva's and she gave me lunch. She kept on about Ada while she mixed up the tuna.

"Whoever it was left that little boy in the lobby has no idea what she started up. Why pick this building? I knew it would mean trouble for Ada as soon as I saw the police and the TV cameras."

"What makes you think it was a woman? You should say person or persons unknown."

"What are you talking about? It had to be a woman. The MOTHER. Who else? I wonder what she was thinking as she laid her son down. The doctors say he was about two days old so she must have loved him a little. The newspaper said she wrapped him up in an old blue towel. No diaper and not a stitch on him. Not circumcised. I told the police he should be called Moses River because he was found on River Avenue. It's already about two years ago. Who do you think has him now?"

I said nothing. How the hell would I know?

"Open that, will you?" She slapped a jar of new dills down in front of me.

"I don't go to the hospital with her anymore. It works out better this way. The last time I went they didn't want to take her in. The little psychiatrist said I maybe could look after her. That's taking community health care too far. After all, I'm not family. Anyway, you saw, she gets on the stretcher, lies down, and has a nice ride. I'll call up tomorrow and talk to the doctor, if he doesn't phone me first.

"When Ada gets like this she thinks she's still in Bialystok and believe me, she won't give them a word of sense. They are going to have to give her that needle every month again. She will not take the pills and I'm not here every day to feed them to her. I hope she gets the same doctor. He knows what to do even if he looks like a boy.

"It makes me sick how the Dorfmans treat her, leaving her to rot in that dinky suite. Not telling her about Gerry's funeral. That I cannot forgive. What they learned, they learned from their father, and a *mensch* he was not."

It was hard to believe that Sid and Jack actually buried their brother without telling Ada. They all loved her when they were little boys. When she married Sol, they were two, four and six years old. There's a photograph of all of them, taken the first summer after Ada came to Winnipeg. In 1949. Sol is dignified in a dark three-piece suit; the boys are in western shirts and cowboy hats, their toy guns holstered. Ada looks pretty good in a European sort of way with her big dark sad eyes. She had a nice figure then and her blonde hair was curled under in a pageboy. She seems very shy, not looking directly at the photographer, giving a little smile, her body turned away to the right, almost as if she were going to hide behind Sol. The three boys are standing in front, Sid in the middle with his hands on his six-shooters. Jack's standing on one foot and Gerry looks as if he's going to burst out crying. They all look like regular Canadians except Ada. She's got on those funny lace-up shoes with the thick heels and the little piece cut out around the back of the ankle. Open-toed shoes as made in Poland. She looks sweet but like she fell off the turnip truck from Vladivostok only yesterday.

Vladivostok. No, Bialystok, that's where Ada came from. A textile centre about two hundred miles east of Warsaw. Her parents, Dolly and Jacob, had a bakery on Sienkiewicza, the main street. Eva told me the story.

Germany declared war on Poland on September first, 1939. It lasted two weeks. A week later the Wehrmacht entered Bialystok. They shot Ada's parents on the first day because the SS officer did not like rye bread. He demanded sweet rolls. Didn't he know that white flour was a thing of the past in Bialystok?

Apparently not. Because of Eva's interest in this woman, I am aware of certain facts about her. For instance, I know that pious elderly cousins, Moishe and Gittel Walfish, rescued Ada. When they died of influenza in the winter of 1940, gentiles took her in. They hid her in the country at their farm, where she was the little goose girl chasing after the birds with a little stick. That was good until 1942, when she overnight was no longer a stick of a girl but all nicely filled out by country cream. They were calling her Lotte and she caught the eye of the local Wehrmacht commander, who decided that he needed her for the war effort. She told Eva that he brought her to the mayor's house in Bialystok that the SS had taken over and installed her there as his personal maid. Polish my boots, wash my back, sleep with me. He taught her German and got her good food and pretty things to wear. And he wanted her to become pregnant. To carry on the master race. He was a handsome guy and because she was so blonde, he decided she was really an Aryan, or Aryan enough for him. It's hard to believe when you look at her now, and when you know how crazy she can talk, you wonder if any of her story is true.

One day a cousin of her father's, a rabbinical student who was being rounded up by the SS, recognized her and called out to her on the street. In Yiddish, he called her by name and asked about her parents. The officer was furious, he kicked her and punched her and ordered her into the same transport as her cousin. He spat on her and wouldn't speak to her. She had a real bad time of it because, she told Eva, if you can believe it, she was half in love with the officer and, by this time, had forgotten who she really was. The heartbreaking part was that she was pregnant. The child was born in the camp. Dead in the sixth month and she still looks for that boy. One of the other women took it from her, and Ada never saw it again. She thinks the guards have it.

"She never learned to be a Canadian. She always gets the language mixed around. She calls the garage the house for cars."

Eva handed me a tuna on rye with a quartered dill beside.

"Who wants to remember the names of everything in five or six languages? You don't need it. Nobody needs it."

Eva got involved because she's friends with Murray and Bella Katz. Now they expect her to fill in for them when they go to the lake. So I, who never wanted anything to do with this woman, find myself defending her to my exasperated sister. It's a crazy world I'm telling you.

Ada was a real housewife. Some say that is the true reason Sol married her: to get live-in help and a nurse for those boys. Sure, it was all romance at the beginning, with him bringing flowers every week, whistling *Ochi Choryna*, that old song about the girl with the dark eyes. And her with his slippers in her mouth. She made her own bread, put up preserves, and really knocked herself out for any holiday. Mind you, I know this only through the Katzes. Murray said she even made cottage cheese. She looked after those boys with the complete devotion of a robot.

All went good until her first breakdown. Sol came home from the office to find that she had peroxided little Gerry's hair to a golden orangey colour. That was the first anyone heard about golden-haired people from another planet.

She's a peasant. Afraid of electricity. In this day and age. That's how I found myself early last Saturday morning balancing on a folding chair in Ada's kitchen, changing the fluorescent tubes in the light fixture. Strictly institutional. Very ugly. For this, my sister wakes me and has me drive across town. "It's urgent," she said. "The lights are flickering and I'm afraid Ada's going to take a seizure."

I don't say no to Eva. I don't even argue with her about these things. She has her view of the world and I have mine. She calls. I come. This business of making people happy is so erratic; you can't keep a schedule.

When I look at Ada, she always seems to be shivering, caught in the weedy depths of some nightmare. You can almost see the Angel of Death sitting right beside her. You can imagine her days spent listening to the ticking, the dull reality of that ugly clock. Eva says she is capable of spending a whole day like she's still in the camp, comparing methods for eating bread: all at once or crumb by crumb.

That's the difference between Eva and me. She wants to know all the sad details of Ada's dreary life and I don't. I think the less said the better. If I imagine the inside of her head, I see empty rooms—dark with mould and bitter earth and littered with smashed-up furniture.

Eva says, "Do you want to know the symptoms?"

"NO," I say, but she tells me anyway.

"I'll tell you," she says. "There's derangement, that's what Ada's got. There's premature senility, other kinds of brain damage, retardation, there's hormonal disruptions. Some women never can bear children. There's parasites, anemia, hyperventilation, thready pulse, high fevers, fluid retention, bleeding sores, skin rashes."

"How about blood, frogs, vermin, beasts, cattle disease?"

"Stop. Don't *kibbitz* about this. For once in your life, have a little respect. It's worse than the ten plagues. It's all ugliness, sorrow and sickness, pain and despair. And her first-born is already slain."

It's not what I want to think about on a spring weekend when the weather is warm and beautiful. Already the geese are in their flyway, honking their way north. I'd rather be in Mindy Diamond's arms with my nose in her cleavage. Inhaling that basic smell of her. It's lemons and flowers and her heavenly self. Or I could be out on the golf course. Anywhere but here.

Eva keeps on talking. She says there are those rare people, like Ada, who believe in G-d. I think continually of them so that I can go on. Ada never asks why she was condemned to live with those thoughts, those memories.

I think to myself she's too crazy to even know she's crazy and I say, "She'll get freedom from gravity easier than freedom from this kind of memories."

"She was born unlucky and that's it."
"Better a single day of happiness than nothing at all."
"Do you think she had one?"
Eva shrugs like she doesn't know.
"She used to be Ada Rabinowicz."

Once More with Feeling

Mindy Diamond (neé Kravetsky) was building her wall of mah-jong tiles and she continued to move and align the double stacks in what would be the East wall while Eva Rosenthal (neé Kolin) and Ruthie Halprin (neé Birnboim) discussed the difficulties of keeping a marriage alive. The two women spoke with sober authority. They had a total of one hundred and seven years of matrimonial experience between them. Pearl Fine (neé Rubin) said nothing. Everyone present knew the nightmare she had lived until Jack dropped dead at synagogue.

La Bohème, live from the Met, soared in the background as the players prepared their tiles. Mindy, the only divorcée, tapped her nails in time with Rudolpho's warbling but added nothing to the discussion. Bite your tongue, she told herself. Let Eva talk. G-d leaves me too much on my own, she thought. That's how I got started with her brother

Leon. And that took the pulp out of our friendship.

Eva and Ruthie droned on. Like two Talmudic scholars, they examined today's burning question: Is it more the wife's duty to maintain peace in the home than her husband's?

"Men and women," sighed Eva. "We don't speak the same language. That's what gives us our aches and pains."

"I did everything Sid wanted short of wrapping myself in cellophane," Ruthie said.

"He never asked for that, did he?"

"Never! My Sid was a good boy."

"Who started that craziness with the plastic wrap?"

"Someone whose breasts didn't nurse four children."

"Was it that Martha Stewart?"

"No. Before her time."

"She's too busy for sex."

"She's too busy coming up with new recipes for us to try on our unsuspecting families."

"Yes. Or new ways to use regular foods."

"Or inventing one of those disgusting combinations like clamato. Why not prune and flounder or herring and apple?"

"Is there a Mr. Stewart?"

"Who knows? Anyway, if there is, he won't get it. She's too busy stenciling the driveway or making water from scratch to *shtup* him."

"*Chutzpah* à gogo. She's got *chutzpah* to go."

"Girls," cautioned Pearl, "girls, my ears." At her house, there is no smoking (which is torture for Mindy) and no rough talk. Her list of rules is posted on the fridge.

"I am changing the subject, girls. Mindy, tell us what's new with you."

Mindy shrugged. "Nothing really. I'd like to go on a trip

but I don't know where. I'm tired of Palm Beach and of Florida. I am sick of going places where widows are the majority." No one asked her about Leon Kolin because their affair was not discussed. They knew but they did not say.

It isn't as easy to know what one wants as is commonly supposed, Mindy thought. Leon was constantly asking her to go away with him. He thinks they can do this. Both slip away at the same time without anyone being the wiser. Where are the Lesser Antilles? Nobody she knows has ever heard of them. He wants to stay at a hotel where they have fluffy bathrobes. You're crazy, she said. You always run into someone you know at the Winnipeg airport. People will talk. Yes, he said. They'll be jealous.

Ruthie Halprin knocked over her stacks of tiles as she rushed to enter the discussion. "What about Cuba? My brother Issy says we should go to Cuba this year. I'm … I'm not too sure but Issy says we have to do everything we can for Cuba."

Mindy gave her a pained smile as Ruthie re-stacked her tiles. For twenty-two years, before and after her divorce, she'd worked as a sales associate at The House of China. She scorned clumsiness, a failing she considered unfeminine. She continued to be careful with her wedding china though it was chosen by her ex-mother-in-law who had no taste whatsoever. It was fine porcelain.

"The Communists must try to stick together now since there aren't many of them left," said Eva. It was barely three years since her husband, Solly Rosenthal, had been buried with all the ceremony the rag-tag north-end Party could muster, including an honour guard and a scarlet hammer and sickle flag draped over his coffin.

It isn't easy to know what one really wants. Leon and his

wife, Shifra, did not seem to know what they wanted. Together. Or separately. She'd left Leon to manage their successful kosher catering business while she went to Israel to find herself in the peace movement. And now she was coming home because their daughter, Karen, was engaged again. At least the girl wasn't in the psycho ward this time.

This meant that Shifra would be staying with him at their house on O'Meara Street. Staying in their marital bed. Leon would rocket back and forth between the two of them. For five years, before and after Harold left her, even before Shifra went to Israel, he was sneaking down the back lane from his house. This infuriated her. Leon swore that Shifra did not suspect a thing. That meant that he did not have to choose. At least to his way of thinking.

Make up your mind. You're the doctor. Mindy remembered shouting those words at him that morning before she turned her face into the pillow.

Some days she told herself that she did not care whether he decided to follow Shifra to Israel or not. Half the time she believed he would, though he did not share his wife's interest in the peace movement. He had no interest in anything but the stock market.

She told him what Pearl Fine said. Three things drain a man's health: worry, travel and sin.

"So Masha, now you're a philosopher, a Talmudic know-it-all. Tell me, does this feel like sin?"

He leaned over and kissed the last visible bone in her spine. His breath feathered down the cleft of her buttocks.

"If you're worried about sin, you'd better leave me." He began gently massaging her back. "No tears, darling. I'll talk to my sister. Eva can speak to Ruthie Halprin. I'm pretty sure her brother Issy is available."

"I've been playing maj with Ruthie every Saturday afternoon for thirty-five years. I hear plenty about that brother of hers. I know enough about Israel Birnboim. Thanks, but no thanks."

She had seen Issy's feet out at Winnipeg Beach. Clay-coloured on egg-smooth stones that matched his pale egg-like head. A head precariously balanced atop his massive body. There's over six feet of it; his trunk tilts forward slightly as he prowls the aisles of his deli on short legs, surveying boxed goods and tins. He has a good word for everyone who walks through the door.

Leon had no idea that she had gone on a dinner date with Issy. Or how he had tried to act the big shot! Reserved for that fancy French place in St. Boniface where the service is slow—on purpose. When the waiter came to their table, Issy asked him, What is my crime? The waiter didn't understand. Then Issy pulls on the guy's sleeve and says, well, there must be something: you've had me on bread and water since I came in.

I should fall in love with this? she said to herself and dismissed his requests for other dates by saying she was not ready to start up again.

She saw that Leon was pulling up his trousers. He looked over but she stayed curled up, under the duvet.

"How can you women play that silly game week after week?"

"We play maj because it's easy and you can talk and eat at the same time. Like those sports you men go for, bowling and pool. Where you can drink beer and smoke cigars while you play."

He reached over to caress her right breast.

"Not now." She turned away from him.

"Mindy! What does *not now* mean when you're over sixty? Time is flying by. I still feel like I'm forty years old. Then I look in the mirror and ask *who* the hell is that? I know what I want! I want something that involves the five senses. All of them. I want to feel like I'm in love again."

"Why don't you leave now? Go walk your dog. Go home to wait for your wife. I can't talk to you. You give me a headache! I'm so sick I can't talk to myself."

"I HEAR CONGRATULATIONS are in order." Mindy looked knowingly across the table at Eva whose pale lips were pursed in concentration as she considered her tiles. "So let me be the first to say *mazel tov*! I hear that your niece Karen is engaged."

"Give me double *mazel tov*. He's not an Israeli."

"Who then?" asked Ruthie.

"Who knows how these things happen? But it so happened that she had to go all the way to Israel to visit her mother to meet a boy from the south end. You know the Golds from Tuxedo?"

"Which?"

"Alan and Naomi."

"The jeans people?"

"Them. Their middle boy, Kerry."

"Is he in the family business?"

"Yes. *Schmates*."

That's some merger thought Mindy. The social notice in *The Western Jewish News* can read "Western denim marries Delicious Foods."

"I hear he's a nice boy," offered Pearl.

Mindy thought he'd have to be more than nice. Strong would be better if he were going to marry with that Karen and her problems. Leon would gladly pass responsibility for her on to Kerry Gold. Talk about giving away the bride.

Last week, with the news of the engagement fresh, Leon tried to convince her to rent a condo in Palm Springs for the winter. When she mentioned Karen's name, he let loose a shocking mouthful of curses.

"How can you speak that way of your daughter?" she demanded.

"Sorry." He flushed and looked away.

"If it's in you, it'll get out."

"Where, I want to know," Leon continued, "is it written that you must love your children? Or vice versa? The Ten Commandments speak of honour, not love.

"Here, pick up the phone. Dial 284-6644. If she answers, she's still alive.

"Busy? Yeah, that's no surprise. Miss *Dreykop*'s got a stranglehold on the phone."

"Does he know? Does he know about your daughter's mental problems?"

"Who can tell? He's too busy locking the horns on his head into the holes in hers." He pulled her close to whisper in her ear, "Every Paradise has its serpent and she is the snake in our garden."

Mindy often wondered how things would work out for her and Leon if the way were clear for them to be together. It isn't as easy to know what one wants as is commonly supposed. Even for those who say, all I want is to be with you.

NEITHER OF THEM EXPECTED that events would unfold in the way that Shifra arranged. She rang Mindy's doorbell the following Sunday evening and invited herself in. She took a seat on the sofa and leaned back against the throw cushions, exhaling a sickeningly sweet medicinal odour that made Mindy gag.

Shifra reached inside her blouse and adjusted the prosthesis that sat where her right breast used to be. "Excuse me but this thing is so itchy in hot weather. It reminds me. In case I should ever forget. You look at yourself in the mirror and think—I have cancer. I had cancer. But the tense keeps slipping. I have cancer. I had cancer. I have cancer again. I will always have cancer. It's death on the installment plan."

Shifra had never been in the house before unless you count that one time she came campaigning for the Israeli war orphans. Mindy couldn't figure out what she wanted. Talking about her cancer. It made Mindy sick and besides, it was public knowledge. Another reason she gave for moving to Israel.

Shifra cleared her throat, crossed her plump sleek legs and patted her linen skirt down over her knees.

"Mindy, this need not be awkward," she began. "After all, I think that you know, that I know, that every time Leon took our dog for a walk he was sneaking down the back lane to visit you on a regular basis for the past however many years." She cleared her throat. "I'm willing to overlook that. In an odd way it has begun to feel that you are part of our family. I suppose that sounds strange but that's how I see it. So we are in the same *mishpokhe* then. Not even considering that my cousin Bernie married your cousin Freyda and anyone could say that qualifies us as family too. No matter what you think, I feel close to you.

"Don't look so stunned, Mindy. You never know what role you play in other people's lives. There's nothing you can do about it. Take that cross look off your pretty face.

"You heard, I think, from Eva at yesterday's maj game that my Karen is marrying Kerry Gold. The wedding was originally planned for next June. Recently I found out that my cancer has returned and I'm considered terminal. So we've had to make adjustments in all our plans."

She held up her hand for silence. Mindy wanted to say something, but her lips forgot how to make words

"I've been told to put my affairs in order. The house is in my name. It belonged to my parents. I want to be sure it goes to Karen and Kerry so Leon has to get out now. Before the wedding. I'm sick of looking at him. I've arranged for a truck to bring his things to your house tomorrow. I think it's time you got to know Leon.

"Don't look so shocked, Mindy. You won't have to do anything. I'm willing to spend one of my last afternoons sitting at the rabbi's while he writes out our divorce."

"Do you think it will work out for us?" Mindy asked.

The sour look on Shifra's face indicated what she thought.

"I'm the Queen of Optimism. I'm on Cloud Five. Let's sell the herring and schnapps farm and move to the city." Her face showed weary resignation. Apparently Shifra was determined that Mindy understand what she did not know about Leon. How careless and demanding he was. The daily physical details: the mess he left in the sink when he trimmed the hair from his ears, his black moods, the gambling. She was leaving her husband to Mindy in "as is" condition.

An hour later Leon turned up at Mindy's door. He looked pale beneath his golfer's tan.

"You heard?"

"She came over. She didn't tell you?"

"She told. She told me good."

Shifra had told him to pack his shaving gear and get over to Mindy's. The movers would bring the rest of his stuff in the morning. He went to the bathroom for his razor. He looked at himself in the mirror. He was tired. He ran his hand over his chin. He looked old. Like he was turning to ashes already. His five o'clock shadow faded to grey. He stared into his own eyes and in his mind, Eva shouted at him *you cheat, you louse.* He sat down on the toilet lid and let his eyes mist over. His hands were shaking so he had trouble using his electric razor. He was going to be in the doghouse with Eva. He thought of all the mistakes he'd made but failed to recall what was the first. Did he make a wrong answer to some question that he thought was unimportant? He had no idea.

"Do I have to stand here on the doorstep?"

"What a stupid question. Are you going to live here or not?"

He smiled and ran his tongue along his top lip under his moustache.

Mindy thought he was like the cat that got the cream. A stray. A tomcat that could be given away without a pang. That Shifra was a little general, giving everyone orders. The whole Kolin family was nutso.

She screamed at him, "Karen isn't the only one with mental problems. You are. Your wife is. Your whole family is *meshugge.*"

"Sweetie. You look tired. Let me hold you. Didn't you sleep well last night?"

"I couldn't sleep. It must be the knife in my back. Why is she doing this to us? She can't leave her husband to someone like he was a piece of property. What will people say?"

"Who cares? I said I'd move to keep peace in the house. After she's dead, things will be different. I promise you. Karen doesn't want the house. I'm not trying to figure out why Shifra wants us to be together. She wants it this way and that's good enough for me. We can be happy at last."

"No." She moved out of his arms. "No. We can never be happy this way. She has to die and make you a widower first. If we agree to live together now, it'll be unforgivable. Her cancer is getting in between us. It's crushing us. Her unhappiness and Karen's. Why should I have to suffer for her? Then it's like in maj. She's the winner. She Goes Out and I have no more chances. No. I won't do it."

Leon ground the palms of his hands into his red-rimmed eyes. His head ached with new questions. He wasn't sure their love could survive this new freedom Shifra had granted.

"There's no reason to wait. She as good as gave us her blessing." He pulled her into his arms. What if she knew that all he was thinking about was burying the thick hard root of himself deep inside her to hush that shrill impatient mouth.

"It's no blessing, you fool. It's a curse. Our trouble is only beginning. And you're so willing to do for her, you don't see it." She pounded on his back with both fists. "You might as well be her dancing dog."

Wrap Your Troubles in Dreams

GRETA JORGENSON'S FINGERS ACHED. SHE'D BEEN
crocheting for almost five hours, sitting on a backside-
numbing orange plastic chair off to the side of Teddy's hard
bed. All that time, he lay quiet on the sheets, surrounded by
blinking machines with complicated-looking dials,
anchored to the bed by plastic tubes that fed him pale
coloured liquids or carried darker ones away. This place
looks like Star Trek, she thought. Looks like he's waiting for
his old friend Spock.

For two days, she sat motionless as a fly can, with one ear
tuned to the soft hypnotic click and whoosh of his ventila-
tor and the other to the coded phrases of the tired-eyed
staff manning the elevated command post in the centre of
the room. "How are his lytes?" "Let's get LFTs and a CVP
stat." They checked their computer screens for new
coordinates, analyzed the data, revised the mission's plan.

Trying their level best to beam their patients up. She knew that they weren't going to get Teddy back. His lights were punched out. But she didn't say a word, she'd seen how they hated failure.

Greta decided to go downstairs to sit in the Quiet Room. She wanted to avoid the crowd in the family waiting room. The air in there was thick as fog and made her shiver when she thought of what they said on the TV last night about Saddam Hussein and his poison gas. It was about the only place in the hospital where you could still smoke. And it was packed tonight with a real smoking crowd. The air was throbbing with emergency prayers and dark feelings those people were breathing out. Waiting, pacing and thinking about the one they loved who was tethered to a fancy bed in Intensive Care.

Greta settled her square shoulders back against the dark brown vinyl of the couch and, because she was alone, slipped off her pumps and anchored her heels on the tower of battered magazines piled up on the arborite coffee table. That felt comfy. Taking a load off.

Except for the Christmas decorations, every detail of the room was exactly as she remembered from two years ago. Pale peach walls, a painting of windblown trees called the *West Wind*, the sticker above the dial on the phone: For Chaplaincy service dial extension 3462. The doctors had brought her here to tell her that Emil wasn't going to live. He got hurt trying to haul his damn old shingle-splitting machine up into the barn with the small tractor. It reared up like a spooked gelding and pinned him to the ground, crushing his chest. The younger doctor with the brown cow eyes (Jewish, she thought) solemnly took her hand and explained the things: extensive damage to the rib cage, lacerated lungs, bruised heart. The things that were too much to be borne.

Now it was Teddy's turn to keep her waiting for the bad news. She recognized only a handful of the nurses and all the doctors were different. That was a relief. It was hard to lie, even to strangers. She kept telling them that she didn't know what had happened to him and that was as close to it as she could get.

Greta thought about the first time Teddy tried to kill himself. Last February. Right after she and Charlie got back from a weekend fling in Vegas. She had been in to Steinbach to see Donna, her hairdresser, for a perm, and she was feeling pleased with the way it turned out. It gave her thin blonde-streaked hair extra body, just like Donna promised. Donna had talked Greta into having her eyebrows arched too. Not that any of this made her into a great beauty at age forty-nine. It was her father's idea to call her Greta after the great Garbo. He was crazy about "Ninotchka." He was surprised when his daughter grew up into a long-limbed, square frame with a face as flat as a plate and as white as the moon.

When she got back home, she lingered in front of the hall mirror to inspect the effect of her new lipstick (Watermelon Glow). She felt a twinge of worry that she'd got rooked out of $10.98 for that stick of goo because she believed the Mary Kay saleslady's claim that it brought out her natural facial tones. She was singing softly, "Just remember that sunshine always follows the rain, so wrap all your troubles in dreams and dream all your troubles again . . . ," twisting and poking at her new curls. She knew she didn't have all the words right yet; her interest in Frank Sinatra was as new as her love for Charlie Penner. It took a

few minutes for it to dawn on her that she couldn't hear
Teddy's television set blaring. He had a thing for black
women and was usually watching the Oprah Winfrey show
about then. It was nearly three o'clock.

Her whole insides began to shake like a jelly salad. She
had to force herself to walk back through the kitchen into
Teddy's room. He slept out in the addition (a bedroom with
its own bathroom) that Emil had put on the summer after
Teddy was diagnosed with having the sugar diabetes right
before his sixteenth birthday. The room was built as part of
the plan made up by the team at the Children's Hospital in
Winnipeg to get Teddy to accept his illness and become
independent. The whole thing was a damn flop and he
went right ahead with his wild sprees, drinking beer and
tearing up the countryside on his motorcycle until he broke
a leg trying to jump a culvert. Four months in the hospital
for that escapade. The little fool liked to think he was Evel
Knievel.

Teddy was lying face down on the floor with his shaved
head resting against the frame of his waterbed. There was a
wet spot on the broadloom right by an overturned beer
can. It was a "lite" brand, the only allowance he made for
his illness. His red telephone was upside down and the cord
was twisted around his left ankle. All he had on was a
smelly old pair of Levi's, hanging down so low she could see
the crack between the white globes of his ass. His neck was
twisted around and his eyes were partway open so he
looked like he was staring over his left shoulder. A dried up
trail of spit or vomit meandered across his chin. His filthy
fingernails were beginning to curl under and his skin was
all dull and flakey. Greta saw that Charlie was right. Teddy
was beginning to look like Howard Hughes. She bent down

and rolled him over. His breathing was so shallow she thought he was finally gone.

What else was Charlie right about?

Everything seemed definite when he spoke in his rich salesman's voice, singing a melody so chock full of confidence that he could make even bad news sound promising. Greta once told Charlie that he'd make a great preacher. Not on your life, he said. He pretended to be shocked, like she'd suggested that he take up a life of crime. To his mind, preachers were all lowlife Hallelujah pickpockets, and he claimed professional wrestling gave the good and evil message in a far more entertaining way. He let on how he was kind of interested in politics, though, and said if he hadn't already put himself out to pasture, he'd consider it. But, hell, he'd got his whole retirement planned out and it didn't include jawing with a bunch of strangers over feed subsidies and yield forecasts. "Anyhow, they don't need me," he joked, "there's no shortage of fertilizer in this part of the country."

The trouble between Teddy and Charlie began the moment they laid eyes on each other. At first, Greta was too nervous to tell people that she'd run an ad for a new husband in the *Co-operator*. She would never have dared it on her own. She was egged on by Donna, who said that there was no shame in it, everybody was doing it these days. Teddy made barnyard jokes about the letters she got. He managed to scare off a few callers over the phone by telling them that they were required to bring a semen sample, or by pretending to be Greta's boiling mad husband. Charlie saw right through these little tricks and outright ignored Teddy.

The first time Charlie kissed her they were standing outside the Pancake Place at lunchtime on last January fifteenth. In the west, the overcast sky was thinning out, arching up in front of a chinook. "There's a thaw coming, Greta," he announced. "Take a good look, it's headed our way." Then he grabbed her and gave her a generous kiss. Later, he claimed he was hypnotized by a ray of sunlight that glanced off the gold initial G on the lower edge of her tinted glasses. She loved his joshing, his insisting that she was some red-hot mama. Two weeks after, he showed up at her door with tickets for that weekend trip to Vegas. "Oh, live it up with me," he sang. "Live it up with me, my lovely Olive."

"He says it so easy," she complained to Donna. "Always hurrying me on his way." She was thinking of the lists she'd made of her good and bad points, canceling them off against each other. Didn't seem like she had enough pluses to support her dreams.

"Go on down to Vegas with him," Donna insisted. "Honey, don't you even think about it. You only get to go around once, might as well have some fun before you wind up cooking in another man's saucepans. And don't worry yourself over much. Listen. When a guy is in the mood to jump all over your bones, he don't look for flaws. Stick with the tried and true: get yourself some black undies and cold vodka and you'll have no problems.

"And don't you worry about Teddy. He'll make out all right on his own. He's got to learn how sometime, he's over thirty years old now." She shook Greta's blonde trimmings off the cape with an almighty loud snap. "It's past time actually."

On the plane on the way down, Charlie pushed the armrest up and snuggled right up to her. "Look, Olive," he said, running his broad freckled hand up her leg from knee to crotch, "even our thighs match. Inch for inch, a perfect fit.

Stick with me, baby, and you'll never be cold at night. I'll take care of every little thing," he crooned. "I'll be your Popeye the sailor man. Always strong to the finish." He gave her leg a squeeze right up at the top. "Toot, toot."

She listened to the stewardesses talking as they neared her seat, threading their tiny booze cart down the narrow aisle. "Darling, I need some more *bambalucci*," said the busty blonde one. The dark-haired one, who looked like she really could be Italian, passed her some ice. "*Prego, signora, prego*." The words fell on Greta's ears like strange and beautiful music. She sat up straighter so she would catch every note. Never before had she heard Italian spoken and it dawned on her that if she wanted to, she could probably learn it. The door to a brand spanking new life was opening wide in front of her. She could see clear blue, right through to the horizon. She glided forward, smiling like a fool, her feet sprouting wings.

Life with Emil Jorgenson had been bare of such surprises. He was a good provider, with a sharp eye for livestock and a taste for simple pleasures. Greta married him right out of high school and never regretted a day of their life. On their half section the seasons rolled round like they should and a strong rhythm governed every hour. The corn and hay grew; their cows gave sweet milk. Everything they put their hands to thrived, except their son. After Emil died, Greta couldn't make up her mind to sell the land, though she knew Teddy would never be able to run it. She agreed to rent it out to Jake Hudyma, who farmed next to them. He wanted to try his luck with canary seed.

Loneliness can wake you up. It can make you think you're dying even when you're not. That's how it had started with her. Heaving her up out of a safe dark sleep in the middle of her night. Sixteen months from the day she buried Emil, Greta walked into Donna's shop and asked for a makeover. She couldn't figure out any of the advice she read in beauty magazines, all she knew was her fear that she would always be dismally alone, while every day more of the juice drained out of her. Stuck with spending the rest of her life with women. Passing out bags of Scotch mints to the old folks in the Home with Alberta Buchholz and the Legion auxiliary. She did not want to get used to it.

Donna had suggestions to improve Greta's whole life. Right off she said, "I know what part of your trouble is and don't feel one bit bad about it, but ..." and she trained a critical eye on Greta's blushing face, "I can see that you have a fear of makeup. It's all right, honey," she smiled, "lots of girls do."

Donna herself had no fears in that department. Her hair was a different colour practically every month of the year. At forty-two she was lean and dollface pretty thanks to fine, unlined skin and what she called an upbeat outlook. As a professional beautician, she believed her business was recognizing potential. It's a calling, really, was how she put it.

She struck you like the revved up, wild sort of woman who could easily have two divorces before she hit thirty, but Donna was Mrs. Average. Married at sixteen and for the past twenty-six years to Vernon Laflamme, a local guy who hauled feed for a living. "He's the salt of this earth, my Vern," she told Greta, "but I tell you that job of his has been our salvation. It does take more than enough to keep the fire of romance burning when you are always tripping over your man's dirty socks. When Vern gets home for his long layover every two weeks ... well, I make it worth his while, if you get my meaning. Having him around all the time would be like having the full moon in the sky every night. It'd kinda spoil things."

It was Donna who came up with the idea of going into Winnipeg to consult the psychic. She was driven to distraction over her youngest son, Tom, who was stationed over in Qatar providing security at Canada Dry base one. Donna hated every minute of the three months he'd already put in. The TV at her beauty shop stayed tuned to the cable news, and none of her regulars had the nerve to complain about missing her favourite soaps while captive under a pink plastic cape. It wouldn't do to rile Donna up when your head was in her hands. It was upsetting to see her get cross with Saddam, prancing up and down behind the chairs and taking mighty swoops at the air with her styling shears.

She had it in for the military, too, on account of some drug they'd given to Tommy. Made his blood run thin so he'd be able to stand up to the desert heat. It left him in such a weakened state that when he got his leave at Christmas, he spent most of it wrapped up in a sleeping bag and shivering in front of the fireplace. The military did not even have the courtesy to tell her what the hell it was. Heads will roll, she promised, if I find they've harmed my boy.

Donna led the way through the lobby, which was done up in grey veined marble and old oak they stopped to marvel at (you don't see that kind of quality these days). It was peaceful as a church. As they rode up ten floors in the rickety brass elevator cage, Greta tried to steady herself— I'm taking the lift, she thought. It's just like in the movies. She got the crazy feeling she really was going to consult a higher power and she stood up a little straighter and tried to organize her thoughts so the woman would be able to see what her questions were.

They found themselves outside a locked office door with a large window of frosted glass. RING BUZZER TO ENTER was printed in red ballpoint pen on a torn piece of grey cardboard taped above an ordinary doorbell. Donna advised her not to give too much about herself away to the reader, otherwise they wouldn't be able to tell if she was any good. Greta promised to remain a blank slate.

A sulky-looking, bald man opened the door and waved them in like a maître d' with a bow and sweep of arm that grazed his beer belly. He hitched up his dark blue jogging pants and growled, "Youse can have a seat and wait here. She's gone into overtime again," nodding toward a second door.

Two elderly armchairs upholstered in wine red plush were stationed in front a large-screen console TV. Humphrey Bogart was talking about the Germans and passports to a French policeman with a thin moustache and a smirky kind of smile. Then a crowd of people in a nightclub all stood up and sang a loud song in French. Most of the pretty women were crying.

The blurred voices behind the door stopped and right away a thin, blonde woman came out. Little rivers of mascara trailed down her cheeks. She pulled on a dirty pink ski jacket and banged out the door.

"You go in first," offered Donna.

Greta started out of her chair as the reader appeared in the doorway. "Come on," the woman urged. "Come on in." She limped around behind a beat-up wooden office desk and squeaked her rear end down on a swivel chair fitted out with ruffled cushions in a Holly Hobbie print. The chair groaned like a sick old man.

"What do you want to ask?" she began. "Sit back, relax,

empty your mind." She clamped a long empty ivory cigarette holder between her lips and cleared her throat lustily. "Try to concentrate on your question."

Greta watched the reader's gnarled fingers shuffle a worn deck of ordinary playing cards. On the index finger of her left hand she wore a silver ring with a large pale turquoise stone. It looked like a robin's egg cut in half and exactly matched her round lashless eyes. Her hair was skinned back in a bun but at her hairline Greta could see how her orangey red dye job had grown out to reveal snow white at the scalp.

"I can't make up my mind what to do next," Greta mumbled, twisting her finger where her wedding band used to be. She stared at the green desk blotter.

"Your husband gone?"

"Yes. My Emil died two years ago June," Greta admitted. All her resolve quit her then, and she felt her mind open itself to those clear blue eyes.

"You had a good marriage. I can see lots of happy times," the reader began. She saw two men. "A younger one with brown colour hair. He's kind of a sickly type and he leans on you too much. Maybe he's not a love interest. Anyhow I see he's a drain on your energy. Seems like you are moving apart. Like whatever there was between you is over." She glanced up and fixed a sharp look on Greta who cleared her throat but did not speak. "Does any of this ring a bell?" Her hands crabbed out across the cards, turning them over and grouping them, waiting for Greta's answer.

I hate him sometimes; I hate his damned suffering, Greta thought, unable to stop the visions that flooded into the bare insides of her head. Teddy, shoulders hunched, his fruity breath smelling and loud, telling her to leave Charlie, that he could be all the man she'd ever need. Hauling out his limp white dick for proof. The silky gown he bought her spread like a stain on the couch between them, blood red and throbbing. Teddy, born again in Jesus. Leaving home to stay over at Rolly Nachtigal's place. Going in big time for prayer sessions and faith healing. Witnessing for Jehovah. Taking his name off the list for a kidney transplant, the one good card he had left to play. Teddy calling down his mother for a sinner, blind paws burrowing in his Bible for some words to save her troubled heart.

Perversion, pervert. Greta turned the words over in her mouth where they thickened and clotted in her throat. Like that fancy fruit Charlie had loved to eat down in Vegas. Papaya. Soft golden flesh that split open to reveal a glistening heart of black seeds.

All she wanted was for Teddy to have something out of this life, any solid thing, a wife, a home, work. The only job that sick little puppy ever had was parading and handing out flyers dressed in a chicken suit in front of the Colonel's. He'd never been a handsome one and, as he sickened, his eyes bulged out like a mackerel, and she could no longer guess what he thought, sleeping or awake. She felt too old and weary for these kinds of troubles and there seemed to be nothing to do but run from them.

She pushed it all down inside her and went back further for memories of him before those wayward ideas got into his mind. When he was young and sweet and all hers, like on a July afternoon when they sat out hulling strawberries on the back stoop, their lips and fingers aflame with juice. Never closer in all the rest of their lives.

"Now the other one is older, close to your age," the reader went on, "a big man. I'd say close to six feet. He's a smooth type. There's something of the Clark Gable look about him, kinda debonair-like. It looks like you two are going away on a trip. I see blue skies all the way."

Winnipeg to Houston, that was 2419 kilometres. Greta looked it up on the back of her map of Manitoba. Charlie told her they'd take Interstate 29 all the way to Kansas City, then veer west and south through Topeka, Wichita, Oklahoma City, Dallas, Houston, Galveston and then it'll be a short hop, he winked, to his RV in the trailer park right on the Gulf. I can see us now, he smiled, lounging on deck chairs, drinking long, cool drinks and sniffing up that warm Gulf air.

Greta could see them too. She'd be wearing the Wedgwood blue cotton sundress she'd bought on sale at Holt Renfrew when she and Donna went to the Portage Place mall. She had known when she handed the money over to the black-clad, toadlike saleslady that she was deter-mined to go off with Charlie. Her hands would not stop shaking. Donna grabbed her by the elbow and said, "I'm getting you right out of here, Greta. You're going over-board. We said we were coming in here to look." She added, for the saleslady's benefit, "She don't get into the city that often."

Charlie was kissing her when the news came through. The phone jangled, but he didn't stop until the seventh ring when he pulled away roughly and snatched up the receiver out of its cradle. "Paradise Motel," he said, "the hottest spot on the Gulf." He paused, then in slow motion, handed over the phone. His lips, covered with a clownish scarlet print of hers, moved hesitantly, "My Lord, Olive, oh, no, Lord."

NO ONE ELSE CAME TO the Quiet Room that evening. Greta was ready for it when the doctors came by after midnight to tell her that Teddy was not responding as they had hoped on account of the massive stroke he took. They mentioned his brain stem functions and different kinds of brain waves and life support systems. Seemed like there wasn't much of her boy left. Only his brain stem was working. Greta saw it rising up pink and glistening, a thick fleshy stalk with a dead cauliflower white bud on top. She'd overheard how they called this condition among themselves. Gorfed. Not a real medical word. She liked it better though. It sounded like something that Spock would say, not in a mean way, just telling the truth about something mysterious no one knew how to fix.

She sat down again at Teddy's bedside and took up his cool stubby hand and since she wasn't certain if she wanted to pray for him to live or to die, she began asking for his forgiveness.

Beef and Pudding

WHEN I SPIED THE POST CARD FROM LAS VEGAS WITH AN X over Caesar's Palace in with the bills and flyers on the hall table, my heart sank.

"Viva! January 8—be there or be square," was scrawled on the back in a childlike hand. It was unsigned, but I knew there was a single possibility. *Return to sender*, I thought. Damn Jack. I put the card back in Brian's pile of mail.

My brother was born the year Elvis came to power. Though it is ridiculous to imagine a possible association between those two events, I don't know how otherwise to account for Brian's passion for the music of his King. It is a fully polished facet of his persona like his receding hairline or his devotion to playing Old Timers hockey. You have to love him for it.

Though brotherly love was not on my mind last January eighth when I got the call to bail him and his pal Jack out of the slammer. I felt like doing murder. Especially since the only explanation he offered was the cryptic statement: *Hey, I got the farm built.*

This here is a real decent fine boy, he added in sleepy Elvis tones, stretching his arm halfway around Jack's immense back. They were arrested for disturbing the peace: specifically for bending spoons at Jimmy's Lunch.

Earlier, in a peculiar demonstration of male bonding, Brian and Jack had their heads shaved. *Take 'er down to the wood,* they urged old Phil the barber. I gather that from Phil's, they kept a noon-hour appointment at a photo studio where they posed for the annual addition to their archives. Two heavy, middle-aged, hairy-legged, now totally bald white men, resplendent in plaid bermuda shorts, floral sport shirts and sandals. On January eighth. Their tractor caps worn backwards this year. *I sez to him, give your chapeau the 180.* A good thing, that. For Jack's cap bore the legend *Moody bastard seeks considerate gal for love-hate relationship. No experience necessary.*

That photo, with the two pals standing at attention, goofy smiles in place, their jointly owned, chipped plaster bust of Elvis on a fern stand between them, was framed and added to their wall of fame in Brian's living room. Said bust was reported to be the source of their troubles.

They began the pub-crawl at noon, as is their custom. By early evening they reached the Casa Mia room, which has, shall I say, mainly a working class clientele. Brian and Jack were dining à la carte on local specialties: pickled eggs, sauerkraut and barbecued pigtails. (*You know what Germans are like—they eat everything but the squeal.*) They were approached by a sometime acquaintance of Brian's who, after offering profuse compliments on their plaster icon, attempted to negotiate its purchase.

Never. Why, that'd be like cutting up Solomon's baby!

The fellow raised his bid to five hundred dollars. *No way.* They were firm. *Nothing goes down in value when you're talking Elvis.*

That's when things got ugly. The other fellow stated that he'd be pleased to double that price if it would rid his bar of two losers and that dead guy and he made a grab for the King, yelling "Elvis is dead" repeatedly.

Brian turned to Jack. They began trading lines from Elvis's movies.

Guess we're going to have to go in deeper.

It is a dark ride.

Well I'm mean to the bone.

You'd have to pop bennies to stay awake.

If you fall asleep on your watch, you could get frostbite.

What do you do for a living?

I usually get paid for singing.

Put a new set of seatcovers on my car ... his colour—yellow.

Then Brian said, *It got all spooky and silent and I could hear the wind moaning around. It made the back of my neck all tense up like when you know your old dog is got to be shot and you don't want to be the one to do it. Then ...*

I had had him by the gurgler, Jack chipped in. *And I popped him. Right between the eyes.*

The guy went down like a sack of wet cement and we high-tailed it out of there.

They reenacted the King's birthday celebration evening for me from that first blow to the demonstration of their prowess in spoon bending, ending with a chorus of their anthem:

The record shows, I took the blows, I did it my way.

I MAY NOT APPROVE of their antics but, as Mr. Trollope said, We are all of us responsible for our friends, fathers-in-law for their sons-in-law, brothers for their sisters, husbands for their wives, parents for their children, and even children for their parents. We cannot wipe off from us, as with a wet cloth, the stains left by the fault of those near to us. The inkspot will cling.

I LEFT THE MAIL on the hall table. As I climbed upstairs to my rooms, I felt that familiar late afternoon sadness creep across my mind like a lengthening shadow. I stretched out on the bed and let it have its way with me. Enervation has come to feel like bliss and I welcome it.

I'd had a satisfactory day trip with my pal Christa on the Graduates Club Christmas outing. And though it was sleeting the whole time, no one complained. We toured four art galleries and at each stop the curator gave a talk. Refreshments provided. So we floated on a seasonal current of white wine. Our last stop was an exhibition of photographs celebrating the male nude. When Christa said the air was alive with pheromones, Donnie Parker, our local hotshot realtor, grabbed up the ends of her scarf, inhaled deeply and began pawing the ground. Whoops of laughter rewarded him though he needs no encouragement.

The air was close on the bus, a raw mix of new Christmas scents with a persistent undertone of wet wool I associate with awkward kisses in the grade school cloakroom. I kept that observation to myself; it's the sort of lighthearted remark I put by to share with Robert. When I see him.

It was so lovely and quiet in the house just then, I put

some Schubert lieder on the player. It always calms me. He, too, died young. At thirty-one.

I ran a hot bath to take the chill off and lowered myself down in it until the back of my neck rested on the rim of the clawfoot tub, my breasts, belly and kneecaps forming an archipelago of neglected territories in a foamy ocean.

Is there a twelve-step program for endomorphs that are resigned to their fate? For those of us who never consider body sculpting, whose extreme distaste for the fascistic precludes their participation in aerobics? I'm stout. Or as the French have it: *je pris de l'embonpoint*. As I understand it, that means in good condition. Some ideas are better conveyed in a foreign tongue.

I knew Brian would not put his key in the door before three in the morning. Too late for talk. He habits are crepuscular. He rises at four, has his oatmeal, drops in to the Army and Navy to shoot a few games of snooker, then saunters over to his restaurant to supervise the evening rush and call his bookie.

I like the arrangements Brian and I have now. We each have our own rooms in the duplex built by our grandfather, who was the postmaster here in Waterloo. Situated on a deep lot, the far boundary marked by a trio of red maples, it has sheltered four generations.

Our lives are similarly compartmentalized. I am a Trollope scholar and Brian is a scholar of trollops. Since the accident. I admit that is less than a fair description and I know I should not speak ill of my brother when he, of all the people I know—the one most capable of joy—is inextricably bound by the romance of grief.

On a mean November night fifteen years ago, a forgotten jellied salad changed our lives. It was Dad's birthday dinner and to please his only granddaughter, Jane, he volunteered to drive Brian's wife, Linda, back to their apartment to retrieve the lime-green jello fish with its blind wheel of carrot eye.

The Chev hit a patch of black ice. Brian has not driven since. He walks uptown to his restaurant and he takes a cab anywhere else. He has a charge account with the local company. You cannot speak of Linda or Dad with him.

"Let him be," commands our mother. "I thank God now that your brother quit school to open that pizzeria. So I said it was crazy then. Who thought people would pay for a slice of cardboard with tomato sauce and a dribble of chewy cheese? Your brother is a man of vision; he had the first expresso maker too, don't forget."

What I do not forget is the way we lived then, stumbling over dolls, trying to mind a milk-besotted Jane. That first summer Brian went off to work on a grain freighter as soon as the seaway was open. That's where he met Jack Lachance, seaman, first class.

Throughout the early months of her grieving, Mom smoked and sobbed over daytime TV. I'd come in from class to find her flopped out on the couch: our Regina, languid as a rag doll, Dad's striped terry bathrobe her widow's weeds.

Jane grew up playing house on the carpet while Mom floated on that godawful green brocade sofa, littered with saltine crumbs and surrounded by a myriad of cups with dregs of cold milky tea. Adrift on her sea of melancholy. It was shocking the way she'd call Jane over to get a kiss, pleading, saying her little kisses were all that kept Nana going, and as soon as she'd got it, asking Jane to change the channel for her. All of Jane's dolls were named for characters from the soaps: Laura and Luke and Dr. Tom Horton (a sweet Teddy in napless black and white velvet, shiny as an old tuxedo).

There is great comfort in melancholy. To wallow under its spell with eyes bleary, cheeks red from salt, is permissible so long as the retreat from everyday cares does not rule. As Mr. Anthony Trollope cautioned, sorrow should bar no joy that it does not bar out of absolute necessity. Never be nursed into activity, as though it were a thing in itself divine or praiseworthy.

She never listens to me anyway.

With spring and the changing light came Regina's declaration that she was watching too much TV. She knew this, she said, "for when I look away, I see a black rectangle on the ceiling." With that, she entered her abandoned kitchen and expertly peeled up five pounds of potatoes, while whistling "Them There Eyes." And she was only mildly off-key.

She tiptoed back into the social world, beginning with card playing evenings at the Knights of Columbus hall. Eventually she joined a square-dancing club and found comfort in that good-hearted, wisecracking company, mastering the wacky lingo and formal dances: reels, quadrilles, and the schottische. In she'd come from an evening's practice, blithe and girlish in her excitement, and eagerly demonstrate her footwork on the kitchen lino, holding armfuls of crinoline aside. She began to desert us for weekend competitions. She was a natural and easily found new partners through catchy little notices she made up for the hitching-post, a bulletin board where single dancers put up notices indicating their availability. There's not a smutty thing about it, she insisted. It's strictly business. Her first partner was a bit more than that, I'm sure. She felt guilty over that liaison and made other romantic mistakes. Guilt scarcely improves one's judgement.

It was smooth going once she hitched up with Claude Trudeau (no relation, but I've got me a cousin Pierre). Monsieur Trudeau was a successful trapper and dowser, lean as a hound with clear, unlined olive skin and dark, limpid eyes. That's the end of my sleep problems, she announced. Every day I find time to worry about that man. This concern was no burden but a joy to her, a chance to move out of the long shadow the accident cast over our lives. Ready, as Mr. Trollope would say, to savour again the beef and pudding of married life.

We did not see much of her after the national competition in Trois Rivières. La petite chou went off to Hollywood, Florida, with her Claude. They turned pro and became instructors on a French cable TV show, dancing at Le Club Canadien to the strains of Henri Broussard and the sweetest music from Montreal. Three months later, a telegram read out for my answering machine announced their wedding. DEAR KIDS STOP CLAUDE MADE AN HONEST WOMAN OUT OF ME TODAY STOP It WAS A REGULAR R.C. DO STOP EVERYTHING ACCORDING TO HOYLE STOP LOVE AND KISSES REGINA AND CLAUDE.

There is no stopping Brian either. Not when it comes to the romantic impulse. He dates bimbo types, the last an exotic dancer named Melissa. He bought her a sea-green evening gown, tight as skin with a fishtail flare of net at the knees. The kind Marilyn Monroe used to slink around in: a mermaid dress. She broke up with him when she found out it came from a vintage clothing store.

Jane helped choose it, an act that precipitated a crisis of

conscience for her, given her rigorous feminist views. The kinds that (still) proscribe your legs be unshaven, the hair in your armpits long enough to braid. I swear she buys her thrift shop clothes in bulk lots—all you can wear for twenty dollars. I love her just as if she were mine.

And I am considered the black sheep of the family. The only one to attend university, I not only earned my doctorate (*The Smiles of Trollope's Women: a guide to character*), I became a tenured professor in the English department. Eileen Connelly, Ph.D. This is regarded as exceedingly odd behaviour in our family. *Alis volat propriis*: She flies with her own wings.

Each of us lost the old faith, abandoned our hapless mutual past and took up some easier doctrine. Despite all, the familial bonds have not slackened. Brian and I never actually wore crepe. I wear black because it is slimming. Jane wears it because she is eighteen. We do not bother much with church or the holidays. No tree at Christmas, and we have just a breast of chicken. This is how death keeps a cold grip on our lives. Little wonder I took refuge in the nineteenth century.

I did not fare much better than the others in the sphere of romance. I fell in love with a married man, the dean of arts, Robert MacCleod. He's a sturdy Celt, a six footer, with hair and beard of a uniform pewter. He has been working on an illuminatus novel for the whole twelve years of our affair. It has to do with a linguistics professor who cracks the great code of all language and patterns of thought that, he claims, are laid down in the brain as we learn to speak. Each individual has these immutable cortical traces, unique as the whorls on our fingertips.

Initially, I found Robert's theories charming. As well, and

call me a Romantic if you will, there was a certain, barely discernible yet inviting air of sadness about him. I saw how his forsaken early dreams lingered in his darkling blue eyes. I longed to put my arms around his thickening waist and lay my head on his chest. I thought I could feel him returning my embrace, his chin anchored on the crown of my head. I was ill with a fever for days.

I could not stop myself from wondering where we would first make love. It was in their marital bed. His wife Judith was at the Mayo Clinic and daughter Angela at camp. What shocked me about it was that I did not feel the least bit wicked. Then. I said that to him, Oh aren't we wicked, but I didn't feel it. As Regina often reminds us, one is not proud of all one's deeds in this life.

And though I swore I'd never be that kind of woman, I lost all my power under his hands. A real fool for Love. I have saved the first messages he left on my answering machine when, like courting birds, we trilled our showy notes for each other's ears. These do not make as tidy a bundle as love letters bound with a satin ribbon, but such is the degraded state of romantic impulse at the fag end of the twentieth century.

Robert is a man whose day is past and from whom no one expects more. His wished-for goal of academic celebrity is daily becoming ever more distant, like a comet bound on its outward orbit. How is a raven like a writing desk, he asks; how is a tenured professor like a tethered beast?

The old dean who scuffs around the halls in tired plaid carpet slippers. I have a lock of his hair. Pure silver.

We share a carefully distilled passion. What it has boiled down to is two dinners per week (committee work) and up to eleven p.m. once each month (faculty meeting). I've listened to endless stories about his wife.

Judith is American born and fancies herself in a harsh exile; i.e., unable to get the *Sunday Times* delivered. How can I say something mean about a gifted person who has a tragic illness, a terrifying disease? I claim it as a mistress's privilege. To be the mean-spirited Other Woman. That's what I tell myself as I sit alone evenings, exploring the geography of memory at my leisure.

She has multiple sclerosis and is now suffering a bad patch, courtesy of the 'flu season. She is hot, her slender body afire. He has told me about these periods when the disease is raging and her skin is burning and she cannot bear to be touched. He sleeps dutifully alone in the guest bedroom. The thermostat in their house is turned back to sixty degrees and he goes about in layers of sweaters.

She's slowly being entombed within her own body, under a spell so potent no kiss can awaken her. I wait in wings, understudy to the wife. It is difficult to give everything the correct metaphorical weight. The figures corresponding to this emotional triangle cannot be written down in simple arithmetic.

He telephones. Today, to tell me that he spent the afternoon writing a letter of complaint to *The New Yorker*. He is deeply offended by the change in editorial policy that has resulted in the publication of advertisements for medications to shrink enlarged prostate glands. He threatened to cancel his long-running (thirty-three years) subscription. I don't mind really, all the crackpot letters he writes; they invoke nostalgia for the days when each successful argument increased his ardour.

My bed is not uncomfortable most nights. I do not wish

to have Robert share it. He suffers from bruxism and it unnerves me so. I cannot bear this aural evidence of his conflicted heart.

Why do you keep on with him? my dear friend Christa asks, trying to jar me from my velvet-lined rut. How do you see yourself in five years' time?

Ten pounds heavier for sure.

Why do we construct our lives around men, I wonder, as I squat to warm myself at the banked embers of our moribund affair and contemplate my envious and rueful love. A certain weakness in my character: a craving for love is my revealing answer. In any case, offers to cherish me have fallen off. And my routines, they are of such comfort to me that I doubt—no, I know that I cannot give up certain small, albeit anxious pleasures, simply because they are certain, for the possible pleasures of some other romance. That is why I feel such a fraud on the outings Christa takes me on. I go along to humour her, to keep her company. I was not made for marriage, beef and pudding.

Christa loves to talk about men. The ideal man. Her list is long and specific. A recipe that calls for diverse personal qualities and other spicy bits she believes constitute *homo mirabilis*.

Modern-day men and women—I support the view that we are in reality two different species. My requirements are simple: he must have a good sense of humour and his thighs should be bigger than mine.

As the divine Anthony T. observed, the risks in marriage are far greater for the woman than the man. For his work, his way of life will go on as before. She enters his sphere of life and, knowing nothing, takes a monstrous leap into the dark, unaware that everything will be changed. I do not like the dark; ergo, I stay with Robert.

On the night in question, a year ago, I was feeling raddled. What with all the upset in being called to post bail for the lads. Of course I made light of it, joking that they must be true knights-errant, as the usual thing was for the lady to be rescued. They did not appreciate the allusion. Brian referred slightingly to dear Trollope as my own Mr. T., in an odious comparison with that American muscle man.

Things went awry when Jack asked if he might speak to me privately. I agreed to this interview because, frankly, I resented the absence of Robert's attention. Not for an instant did I suspect that Jack would use the opportunity to declare his love for me.

When he did, I saw it not as Brian did—a cause for joy— but as an event that had enormous potential for social disgrace. Brian has always been forthright in his opinion of Robert. *Yer perfessor. A lovely couple you make—Mr. and Mrs. Egghead.* And I am Mrs. Egg for short.

Did he want to be able to say that I once had an offer of marriage? What could be better than to see your sister settled with a dear, admired friend? He quite simply did not see that Jack was not a suitable suitor. How could I trust the opinion of a man who thinks playing billiards is a reasonable way to while away the hours between luncheon and dinner?

And Jack is every inch the sailor. When he admitted to "complicated intentions," I had a vision of his dark hirsute heart running rusty with blood. His physique does not inspire the use of superlative adjectives. *Pinguid* comes to mind. He has a tattoo of the man in the moon on his left biceps and he can make him wink! Women love it, he told me, as he removed his shirt to demonstrate.

Sorry, I only date my own species. That's what I should have said. A sentiment that Jane would approve. Or better still, I'd rather swim in nuclear waste. But I sat there, my heart ticking like a clock, and then Jack asked, "How do you spell beautiful? I say it's E-i-l-e-e-n." He looked into my eyes. He said, "Lots of guys like . . . heavier women." He offered a wild and unmannerly litany of my charms. And desire as brief as a dream clouded my sensible thoughts.

How was he suddenly lovable? What small matter tipped the balance and made me consider him? I cannot think. This whole business is nonsensical.

During their long recitation of the events leading up to their arrest, which was told with little brilliance but great humour, Jack said he had looked forward to this visit for six months. That he regards Brian as his true brother. Then he began to cry, and as two cartoon-sized tears coursed chin-bound through his greying stubble, he told us of his journey to Chicoutimi early in December. It was the first time his return had not been marked by a feast of his favourite foods. For this his mama had cried as she lay dying.

No sooner had her corpse been carried out of the house than the quarrels over her china, her jewelry and her mink coat began. While those schemers, Julie and Simone, the ugly sisters-in-law, were preparing the funeral meats, they argued over which of them had the proper skin tones to show off the coat and which of them had done most for Helene in those last days. Jack told us he was silent and went along with his brothers and the wives to see the priest. There he pretended to be suddenly overcome and went back to the house. He took the fur from his mother's closet and rushed over to the undertakers with it, telling him that the family had discovered a note from their father which directed that Madame be buried in her coat so she would never be cold.

Can sympathy approximate desire?

He came to stand behind my chair. *My eyes adored you, Though I never laid a hand on you, My eyes adored you*, he sang, adding *this is the Braille version*, his fingers skimming over my breasts. I liked it and I felt that I was betraying Robert. And when he said *I think my tongue could do wonders for you*, words stopped up in my mouth. Embracing, we looked very much like Brancusi's lovers in *The Kiss*. Squat, eye to eye, foreheads touching.

January eighth, and Jack's annual visit are only ten days away. No. I cannot receive him this year. As dear Trollope said, we would suffer the intimacy of a mutual embarrassment in which each feels that the other is feeling something that once existed. Perhaps only a mutual fascination, which may not mean anything deep or serious, though its effect cannot be ignored. And as always, I believe that Trollope is right.

That Jack behaved badly is certain. However, as my lovely Mr. T. has said, there is nothing a woman will not forgive a man when he is weaker than she. I do not know why this episode still pains me. It is not grief but some other poison. Slow, insidious, unrelenting. I struggle to show no outward sign of suffering. I had my sorrow in my youth and have learned to bear disappointment by degrees.

"Like sands through the hourglass, so are the days of our

lives." How I despise that easy aphorism. *Vox populi* and the egg timer of life: everyone becomes anxious in the last ten seconds and it is not simply the worry about the egg being less palatable . . . I must find something else to do in December. And January!

Though I am no expert on married life, my years with sweet Trollope have taught me that after a couple has dealt with dirty-faced children, with household bills and are thickened to stout oaks, the beauty of it all is not so much in the one loved as in the loving. This does not excuse my foolish yearnings but perhaps it may explain the way we live now.

Except for memory all we have is the present and those who say they have no regrets are either fools or liars. And so we go on together. Steadfast. Robert and I. All he has are contract bridge and me. We'll see each other through.

We go on. Or as Brian says to me, C'mon Mrs. Egg, let's roll.